C

CW00450046

Ronald Sukenick

Cows

Invisible Starfall Books

Invisible Starfall Books
isbooks@chello.at

Ronald Sukenick Edition 07

Edited by Thomas Hartl
Cover and book layout: Thomas Hartl

First Invisible Starfall Books Edition, November 2021

Reprinted with kind permission by the Alt-X Press published by
Mark Amerika, www.altx.com.

For enabling The Ronald Sukenick Edition, I am very grateful
to Julia Bloch Frey (now Julia Nolet, www.juliafreyauthor.com),
widow and heiress of Ronald Sukenick, and the Harry Ransom
Humanities Research Center (www.hrc.utexas.edu), University of
Texas at Austin, housing the Ronald Sukenick Papers 1941-1999.

ISBN 9798758337592 (pbk.)

Cows

The cowboy was really only a part-time rancher and he was worried about plutonium triggers for nuclear bombs.

The investigator was in fact a part-time professor called in by the cowboy on the advice of a friend who'd heard about his expertise in the diseases of goats. Expenses paid, a small fee, at worst it was a vacation. The investigator had never been out West.

But as soon as the investigator got off the plane in Denver and started talking to his host, Jim Vaca, it turned out there'd been a misunderstanding.

Vaca had heard the investigator worked at a branch of Cornell's famous Veterinary School, but it seemed he was doing research at the Cornell Medical School in Manhattan, and that he was a Ph.D. not a D.V.M., and that his investigations ranged from divorce snooping to literary sleuthing and that his special interest was disease and the supernatural in Edgar Allen Poe and he was an expert on ghosts.

Not goats.

Embarrassment. Confusion. The investigator wondering about the next plane back. Then, to his surprise, renewed hospitality. The offer stood. How come?

"I'm not a rich man," Vaca in the cab of the rusty green pick-up, he could have been Mr. Marlboro but the look was more chiseler than chiseled. Crafty. Heading west and north, white peaks sawing into washed blue matched his eyes. "Just a part-time cowboy with a ranch up toward Wyoming, and a part-time auto mechanic with a restoration business in Boulder. But my heart's in the ranch, I got about a hundred head and expanding, I got a lot of money in it and I just leased some more land, when the cows started dying. That's why I was thinking of getting some goats, like a friend of mine is trying. I thought maybe they'd be immune. Or llamas, which is getting big, there was a bunch the last stock show in Denver. Believe it or not."

"Immune to what?"

Vaca didn't answer. Then, "That's the problem. I don't know." Uncomfortable. "Oh, I've had the experts out. Profs from the vet college at Fort Collins even."

"What do they say?"

Vaca sort of grinned. "What don't they say? Do a lot of talking anymore but don't say much at all. Meanwhile I got eleven head dead to here."

"It's not the mutilations?" On the plane a native had mentioned it genre tall story.

"You heard about that," Vaca. "Maybe, if you believe the stories." Looking uneasy. "But it makes as much sense as the vets. One of them profs was thinking Mad Cow Disease. Worms rot the brain, they got it in England. No, far as what I can see they could've just as likely been scared to death all I know. Ever seen a spooked cow?"

"No."

"You don't want to," Vaca.

"By what?"

He squinted, pulled stained stetson down, pulled the sun visor down, needed a shave. Blond five o'clock shadow. Jeans, silver and turquoise buckle, fleece lined denim vest, he looked like the real thing. About three in the afternoon, sun something ferocious from the west. The urban knot unraveled into small spreads, horse ranches, ponds, cotton-woods, black cattle grazing grassy sprawl, mesa slit by zig-zag ravines, hog back formations, layers of sliced stone, gold/brown prairie dipping away, breaking waves of rock running up to thrust of foot hills.

Vaca picked up a CB mike, "Vaca, coming home, any calls?"

"Vet called about the post mortem," from a speaker.

"What they find?"

"Nothing. Ears and tongue gone but could have been scavengers."

"Damn. Anything else?"

"Looks like you got something on that radiation study and a little girl's been kidnapped and killed in her own home."

"How can she be kidnapped in her own home?"

"That's the question. They're waiting on the post mortem."

"See you in five," hung up.

"I thought maybe their immune systems, what with all the plutonium at Rocky Flats. The nuke plant," Vaca. "Though cows around here are doing okay. Aside from glowing in the dark." A kind of shy grin.

Highway edged with prairie dogs upright at their holes, tiny fire hydrants guarding miniature volcanoes. A life-size giraffe peered at the mountains from a roadside roof.

"Taxidermist with a sense of humor," Vaca. "They say his house has two stories, the first and the tall. We'll pass the nuke plant, you won't see it but if it was night time you might see them cattle lit up. Some say that's why the cattle mutilations. To figure how much radiation was getting out."

On the plane the investigator heard how for years on and off they'd been having episodes of dead cows found with ears, nose, tongue and genitals surgically removed, nobody really knew the why what or how. But frequent reports of mysterious black helicopters. Way it was told could have been a joke.

"Yeah, some say ky-oats," Vaca, "but those aren't bites, they're incisions, and I never seen a ky-oat went to medical school. Some say it's a weird germ. Others say E.T.s, which is about as likely. It's a complete white-out to here. But anyways, the cows is just the beginning of the story."

"What's the rest?" the investigator.

"I heard para-military macho initiations, I heard federal research teams, I heard satanic cults with pedophile sex rituals, I heard drugs, I heard just about everything," pushing his hat back, scratching his scalp. "That's what we're trying to find out."

Sudden scab of cookie cut houses across the open range in a vast beige metastasis, "What's that?" the investigator.

"That's a mirage, ignore it," Vaca. "We always go from boom town to ghost town out here, that's the real joker. Right under Rocky Flats."

Huge red slabs of upthrust rock in the left distance.

"The other thing," Vaca, "I guess I could start a prairie dog ranch. Throw in a few cute marmots, panning gold, advertise for tourists. Free kiddie donkey rides, catch your own trout pond. Sway-back horses for the dudes. Skiddoos in winter. Hey."

"You're joking," the investigator.

"What's serious compared to that?" gesturing out the windshield with his chin. "We're the joke."

Cresting an overlook the whole Front Range laid out across the horizon, gleaming white, peaks like ghosts hovering.

"Purty as a pitcher, like they say," Vaca. "Like they say, the mountains don't care."

Off the highway, maneuvering through a fleet of cyclists from outer space, judging by their gear. Muscular jockbodies pumping uphill.

"Or sell the garage in Boulder to support it. Real estate's worth more than the business. Brokers knocking at my door." Vaca had a way of continuing what he said five minutes later. As if he were thinking. "More bikes around here than horses anymore."

The colors of the nearest mountains were white green red. White snow, green pines, red rock.

Edge of town end of a rutted road adjacent an auto graveyard, raw cinder block, galvanized iron, corrugated roofs. A quonset hut ramshacking a collection of car carcasses in various stages. Vaca walked in stiffly not exactly limping more like his whole body was gimpy. Waved hello as two auto surgeons looked up.

"This baby needs a universal," said one. "And a blow job," the other.

His office a stained desk clotted with piles of paper, old coffee containers, jar of pencils, chewed sub sandwich, empty Coke cans.

Sitting down, looking through some mail. Muttering. "Vet fees, I'm telling you. Eating jellied racoon by then."

"You say racoons?" The investigator.

"Yup. Got plenty a those. Mule deer. Ky-oats. Ghost chiefs. Tumble weed. Sage brush. Prickly pear. None of it good for cows. Uh-oh. Here we go." Heading for the door. "Let's go, we got some results."

The pick-up, on the bumper two stickers: SHIT HAPPENS and NOT FROM CALIFORNIA. Pulling out fast, "What results?" the investigator. In the cab, shock lurch wheel bounce.

"Hold on. Encar. Radiation in my cinder block."

"Encar?" the investigator.

"National Center for Atmospheric Research. Kickin shit up at the spread the other day. And they don't guess."

"Guess at what?" the investigator.

"Anything," hitting pavement and peeling out. "My place's smack between wind patterns from Fort St. Vrain and Rocky Flats."

"The nuclear plant."

"Ex," Vaca. "Both ghost plants now. They say."

"What were you saying about ghost chiefs?"

"Chief Left Hand. A Ute. They say there's a curse, once here you never leave. That's the least, you know about Rocky Flats, fires, plutonium pollution, coverups. Well Fort

St. Vrain had to be closed too. Closest plant to it is Cherno-byl. Same system."

A highway on the periphery wind shoving at the pick-up, pushing it almost out of lane, sunlight slamming through the windshield. Onto a winding road up a mesa, a low modernist castle on top, mule deer in the right of way. "Early I. M. Pei my buddy says," Vaca. "Says he screwed up some things because of the wind. The wind's a big player out here. I. M. Paid, my buddy calls him."

"What buddy?" the investigator.

"He works there."

Walked in through a court yard centered on a big foun-tain all boarded up. "The weather around here, dumb-ass easterners, it's like building a fountain in a wind tunnel," Vaca. "And when the Chinook comes through at a hundred an hour . . ."

"Who's your buddy?"

"He's interested in two things. One is computers. They're doing a wind pattern study. Been finding radiation in stuff made at a cement plant toward Lyons."

"Your cinder block."

"Yeah maybe."

"And the second thing?"

"The mountains," Vaca. "Lives up there."

When they found the buddy in his office, though, he was in no shape to talk about wind pattern studies. Pale, un-shaved, rings under his eyes, pacing erratically.

"You look like a ghost, Leonard. This here's a professor from the east. Investigating my cows."

"Listen," Leonard, "they found a friend of mine last night dead up near Sugarloaf."

"Fall off a cliff up there?" Vaca.

"No. O.D. maybe."

"It happens, buddy. Oughta lay off yourself."

"Listen," Leonard. "I'm going to."

"Tomorrow."

"Yeah, tomorrow," Leonard. "Look I'm having a little problem, can I talk to you a minute?"

"About what?"

"I think I know some things I'm not supposed to know."

They went out on a terrace. The inspector could see them through the window, walking back and forth, massive red rock slabs in the vertical background. Leonard waving his hands, agitated. They came in after a few minutes of animated conversation, Vaca looking annoyed. "Let's go," he said. They left without saying goodbye, "Well, call me about it at least," Leonard saying as they went out the door.

"He wants to use some of the grazing land I leased." Back in the pick-up.

"So?"

"So? Nothing."

Back down into town, past red sandstone college buildings and left into a narrow canyon, dark pines, high red walls.

"Where now?" the investigator.

"I loaned my cabin to couple of his friends. He can't reach them. He's thinking foul play."

The road winding around, a swift stream a fisherman casting, cyclopean rocks, massive maroon walls closing in. "I needed to get out of the city," the investigator.

"Burned out?" Vaca.

"Out for good."

"What are you doing out here, moonlighting?"

"Sunlighting. Tired of it," the investigator.

"The city is tiring?" Vaca.

"Tired of the way things are going. For me and people I know. We've been folded in, spun off, downsized, out-sourced, bought out and handed lead parachutes. So I re-structured. I temp. Pick-up college teaching jobs, research for hire, free-lance investigation." He was also a part-time high school sub, a part-time bar tender, a part-time cab driver, a part-time dope dealer, definitely part of the sur-plus labor pool, but he thought it better not to mention that.

"So. Time to recycle?"

"Right," the investigator.

"Well, anything is possible in the People's Republic of Boulder. What the cowboys call it. One time the city gave a marriage license to a couple a queers. Next day a cowboy showed up demanded to marry his horse."

"Maybe I'll become a Stalinist."

"Your timing's a little off," Vaca.

"No kidding. I'm still waiting for the revolution," the in-vestigator.

"Things stink, huh?" Vaca.

"Not counting politics? My ex-wife, my ex-house, my ex-kid, my ex-dog, my ex-investments, my ex-bank account ..."

"Cheer up. Maybe things always stink."

A sharp turn out of the canyon, fast, steeply up. The investigator felt his ears pop. Pines growing out of rocks. Soon they were on a dirt road.

"What's he want to use it for?" the investigator.

"Use what?"

"Your land."

"Air planes," Vaca.

"How come?"

"Because it's flat."

A clearing in the pines, rocks steeply up behind it, the cabin, two or three windows, small entry porch, brownish clap board, stone base and chimney.

"Just winterized it," Vaca. "What's that."

Out of car over to an animal lying in front of the steps, a dog. Dead. "Shot," Vaca. He took out a key. Knocked on the door, "Hello, anybody there?" simultaneously thrusting the key in the door shoving it open, the smell, the floor sticky with blood, one body spread legged on a couch nude waist down, the other curled naked on the floor guts hanging out. At first hard to tell which was the man till you saw one had been emasculated, the bloody parts next to the woman's head. The investigator backed out the door and puked.

Vaca came out in a minute, dead pale. "They been shot too. I think afterward. Because it looks like they near bled to death first."

"Did you know them?"

"Christ, I didn't think a couple of bodies had that much blood in them," Vaca. "Friends of Leonard."

"What do you think happened?"

"Let's go, the phone line's been cut."

Vaca got in the truck, grabbed his CB. "You don't look so great," Vaca.

"Neither do you," the investigator.

Into the mike, Vaca, "Yeah, there's been some killings up Sugarloaf, yeah, meet you on the road."

Bumping down the dirt road, Vaca silent, the investigator his head out the window. After a while the investigator, settling back into his seat, "What are you thinking?"

"I'm thinking how am I going to get that mess cleaned up? Ought to make Leonard do it."

Vaca had to go back with the marshal. He arranged a friend to drive the investigator down to Boulder. The friend talked a lot about the drug scene in the mountains, about isolated little mountain towns especially in winter, things getting ingrown and sour, red necks, mountain men and old Hippies all pissed off at civilization and not liking one another much either, about how Patty Hearst was kept as a sex slave in one of the communes back up there.

"But things get pretty weird in town too," the friend. "This little Miss Colorado child found dead in her parent's basement. JonBenet."

The friend dropped the investigator at the Hotel Boulderado, frontier Victorian, Old West panelling, turn-of-century furniture, lobby surrounded by a balcony topped by high stained glass ceiling. A message was waiting at the desk. "The talk is set for Wednesday. Small group, but I've invited friends. The title is 'Spooks'? Lenna."

In his room tossed his valise on the bed pulled a pad from it, made some notes, looked up, caught himself in the mirror, salt and pepper hair, greying five o'clock shadow, hollow cheeks, tired eyes, nose curved like a beak. Not a pretty picture but it was his. A new species—permanently superfluous man. He called the number indicated in the message, asked her to the hotel for a drink. Their only communication to now had been by Email.

Met her at the desk, chestnut hair maybe thirty in jock-perfect shape but dressed down in sober pants suit, pearls. They went up to the balcony lounge and settled into a maroon velvet love seat in front of a small antiquey table.

"How did you know I was coming?" the investigator.

"Coincidence. An internet posting."

"How come a computer hacker is interested in the supernatural?"

"I thought spooks meant secret agents. Boulder is a spooky town." A little smile. "And I'm not exactly a hacker," Lenna.

"Cyberneticist?" She was pretty, but he was having a hard time paying attention.

"A little pretentious, but okay. I'm with DermoCorp, a division of Multitech. Tell me about your work."

"Well," the investigator, "if you know Poe you know what it's about. Detectives and ghosts." Flippant, edgy.

The waitress came by. She ordered a glass of white. He a Glen Mackchrankie, double. Still tense.

"Actually I've never read Poe," Lenna. "Should I?" Unbuttoning her jacket. Something about her eyes, deep brown, too deep. Victim eyes. Raped, or expecting rape.

"Should?" The investigator. "How do you mean should?" Watching the shape of her breast define itself under her silk blouse he suddenly had the feeling other priorities were about to take hold.

"I mean, what am I missing?" Lenna.

"I'd like to know." Maybe murder stimulates the senses.

She looked at him in another way. Appraising. "You'll just have to guess." A little smile. "Why exactly are you here?"

"It's a mistake. I'm investigating dead cattle. I don't know anything about dead cattle."

"What cattle?" Smoothing her hair it swayed slightly, nippling her blouse.

"A man named Vaca."

"Jim Vaca?" Lenna, the investigator detected a faint blush.

"Why?" the investigator.

"We used to date."

"It must be a small town," the investigator. "You from here?"

"L.A.," Lenna. "Matter of fact it's very big for a small town."

"Meaning?"

"I've heard it called a hot bed."

"Interesting phrase," the investigator.

"I mean very intricate. You never get to know the whole thing."

"Full of surprises?"

"Some days," Lenna.

"Yeah. Well I've already had some. You free for dinner?"

"Sorry," Lenna. "I'm committed to a gathering. Why don't you come along?"

"Thanks, but I need to eat."

Laughing, "Don't worry, there'll be plenty of food. And you'll see a certain side of Boulder, a side some people would kill to access."

"Don't say that," the investigator.

He told her about the murders, went on some. Why didn't she seem impressed?

"Looks like Jim's got a tiger by the tail," Lenna.

"The tiger being?"

"Around here drugs for sure. I don't know. And Jim probably doesn't either."

"Why do you say that?" the investigator.

"Jim gets involved in things he doesn't understand. Jim's old Boulder, there aren't many left. This town intersects a lot of networks now."

"Like Aspen?"

"A lot quieter than Aspen. Happily. What do you know about Boulder?"

"Nothing. The child beauty queen murder."

"JonBenet. They say she was molested before being killed." She shivered. "It gives me the creeps."

When they left it was dark. She had a Volvo P-1800, celery colored, 1966 but like new. "It's how I met Jim, rebuilding it." They drove somewhere, up mostly. He could feel the pull, what he thought of as sexual gravity, when you know you're going to make love with somebody. Sooner or later. Whether you mean to or not. His best advice was not, he was still staggering from his ex-marriage. But it was only advice.

"What's the party?" the investigator.

"We have an international conference going on. People from all over. It's at the university but the action is at night, in homes."

After about ten minutes a lot of swerving. When they stopped they could see the lights of the town, of several towns and their network of roads, laid out as if from an air plane. The same view from inside was framed by a balcony and a glass walled living space where crowded guests served themselves from a lush buffet and chose between an '86 Pomerol and a '91 Puligny-Montrachet. The host was tweedy, genteel, tennis and golf.

"Todd Golden. Mr. Dupenski's from New York."

"You look good enough to eat honey. Howdy," offering a hand. "What kind of name's Dupensky?"

"It's Polish."

"He wanted to know the difference between Boulder and Aspen," Lenna.

"You mean Rodeo Drive East? It's places like Aspen that give the rich a bad name. Besides, we're more left wing than Aspen."

"I thought Boulder was lily-white," the investigator.

"You want spooks?" Golden. "We had a Negro here. Elected him mayor. Excuse me."

Moving on toward the buffet, "He looks very jocko." The investigator.

"What do you play?"

"You mean sports? Sometimes I take the subway at rush hour. What about Golden?"

"He's very serious about fox hunting," a tight little grin. "Red coats and all."

"A lot of foxes in Colorado?" the investigator.

"They use coyotes. Oh hello Ev. This is Ben Dupenski. He's giving a talk tomorrow. Evelyn Childers, one of our conferees."

A mean whiplash of a man, about fifty. "So they've recruited you too?" Childers. "What are you speaking about?"

"Ghosts. You?"

"Spooks."

"Evan spent many years in the C.I.A.," Lenna.

"Doing?"

"Being spooky," Childers. "How's the skin trade?"

"Things are going smoothly," Lenna.

"Well, it can't be too smooth. Too thin, maybe, too dark, but not too smooth." His beeper went off. "Excuse me," heading toward the next room dialing his cell phone.

"He doesn't like to talk about it," the investigator.

"Oh I don't know. There are a lot of intelligence people around this town. Todd was one."

"Retired?"

"Retired, yes. He says you never get out."

"What was that about skin?" the investigator.

"Nothing. I'm working with a project developing pros-thetic skin. The kind of high tech thing we do around here."

"You mean human skin?"

"Yes."

"Try it on lampshades, there might be a spin-off."

"Yuck, what's that mean?" Lenna.

"Hey," the investigator, "hey I know that guy. Lavigne!" A chubby, baggy number with big eye glasses.

"I didn't know you were out here," the investigator. "Lenna Snipe, Sid Lavigne. We were in grad school to-gether. Tenured, I assume?"

"Oh, for years. And you?"

"A little job, a talk, a vacation. First time. You don't know Lenna? She works with skin."

"I bet."

"You explain," the investigator to Lenna. "I'm hungry."

He was very hungry. Filling his plate at the buffet he took it to a table in a corner and ate non-stop while casing the congregation. An heroic air of self-satisfaction pre-vailed, he'd seen it before in preserves of the rich and their pets. Anyway, the food was good, except he couldn't iden-tify some of it, especially one dish that tasted a little like pork but wasn't, probably something too rare for his palate to recognize. Like maybe panda meat. He was almost done when Vaca walked in and spotted him. He'd changed clothes, a corduroy jacket and bolo tie, but looked out of it.

"Hey, I tried the hotel," Vaca. "Who arranged the coincidence?"

"Friend of yours," gesturing toward Lenna. "Any news?"

"Not really," Vaca. "Leonard don't know anything. He says. The cops think maybe drugs."

"Why?"

He shrugged. "Least they got them out of there. It stinks, how am I supposed to clean that up? Probably worse when it dries. Oh jesus," he looked ready to gag. "How'd you run across Lenna?"

"Internet. Here comes our host," the investigator.

Golden greeted Vaca and asked him about his herd.

"You know about that?" Vaca.

"Sure. Anything starts happening to the cattle around here we're all concerned."

"The latest theory is radiation from Rocky Flats," Vaca.

"There's never been any radiation coming out of the Flats."

"That's not what the grand jury investigation said," Vaca.

Golden smiled. "Effem."

"And Encar's tracking fallout."

"Then Encar better be careful. That's an interesting name for a cowboy, Vaca. What is it, Wetback?"

"Redskin."

Golden's beeper went off, he walked away.

"You putting him on?" the investigator.

"Me, ahm jist a lonesome cowboy. Hear he got a big piece of the real estate company developing houses around the

Flats," Vaca. "Shee-ee-it."

"I thought you live here because you like it."

"I don't have to like it. It's just that it sucks less than everywhere else. I'm probably leaving early if you're tired."

"I'll probably do the round trip with Lenna."

"Sure. If you like the company of New Age E.T.s," Vaca.

"I thought she was from the Wild West."

"L.A. ain't the West. Wild, maybe." Looking over at her talking to Golden. "She's turned on by money."

"Aren't we all," the investigator.

The womp-womp-womp noise of a helicopter rose above the noises of the party then drowned them, lights snapped on the terrace outside as it landed in a cloud of dust. A crowd gathered in front of the picture window as a dumpy little man in glasses and camo parka bent against the windstorm of the now ascending copter followed by a big man carrying a brief case and a guy with a pony tail.

"It's just the Colonel," Vaca.

"Who's the Colonel?"

"We don't know. U.S. Army, retired. He's always around Golden."

The Colonel came in ear to cell phone taking a handshake from Golden who escorted him somewhere.

"Does he always arrive in a puff of smoke?" the investigator.

"I couldn't say. They used to say he was here looking for the Unabomber when he was holed up in the mountains. Some said he was trying to catch him some said he was trying to help him."

"Who are the others from the chopper?"

"Maybe they're on the same paint ball team," Vaca.

A husky, rumpled looking guy slouched over, the pony tail from the helicopter, youngish but balding, rimless glasses, what hair he had leaking down his neck held in place by a leather ring. Jeans, cowboy boots, fringed leather jacket over a t-shirt with a grinning skull that said, "KILL 'EM ALL, LET GOD SORT 'EM OUT."

"Hello Trench," Vaca. "This is Trench Fenster, Ben Dupenski. He works for a local publication, "Soldier of Fortune." Maybe you heard of it."

"The magazine for mercenaries?" The investigator.

"Right. Writes for it. Trained by the Creative Writing program at the college."

He didn't look like a mercenary, more like the perpetual Ph.D. candidates that litter college towns.

"How'd you get into the mercenary scene?" The investigator.

"Money. Excitement. Perks."

"What perks?"

"Ah-hah!" He rolled his eyes.

"Trench's from Texas," Vaca. "That explains everything."

"People in Colorado blame indigestion and the weather on Texans," Trench. "I'm used to it. What's this I hear about Golden running for the Senate?"

"Sure," Vaca. "I thought you guys didn't like government."

"We don't, we use it. Besides, why not? He's superrich, good looking, old Colorado. Has government experience,"

Fenster.

"You call that government?" Vaca.

"You bet," Trench. "Intelligence. The most important."

"Well, as long as he gets his goodies probably don't matter what he does," Vaca.

"You think it's that bad?" Trench.

"Ask me, I'm customizing his SL 380 with stash box in the ash tray."

"How do you figure these killings in your cabin?" Trench.

"You saw it in the papers already?" Vaca.

"It won't be in the papers," Trench.

"Then you tell me."

"Hey. You hear," Trench, "they got a can of plutonium waste started vibrating at the Flats, none of their experts has a clue why?"

"Always something. Where'd you hear that?" Vaca.

"Sources. Damn thing moved a half inch last night. But don't worry, they say it's perfectly safe."

"Right."

"Right. Fucking Feds," Trench, "they're too busy defending the squawfish and the razorback sucker to think about protecting citizens. We'll catch up with them like we did in okay city."

"What's okay city?" the investigator. He had the feeling Trench's affability was spiked with something nutty, the sort of guy who could enjoy a good lunch with you and stab you on the way out.

"Oklahoma," Trench, "it's a famous musical. We're composing some music."

Percussive staccato of detonations from outside, the investigator spilled his drink.

"Relax," Trench, "it's just Golden and the Colonel, they like to get drunk and talk about Plan B." Outside on the terrace the two of them with military looking weapons shooting into the pine woods, wine glasses set on low terrace wall. They stopped and lifted their glasses.

"Probably a Ruger Maxi-14 and a Star nine millimeter BM," Trench. "Or maybe an H&K ninety-four nine millimeter."

"What's Plan B?" the investigator.

"Just spook talk," Trench.

Lenna came over to the investigator. "You think you can catch a ride back down with Vaca? Todd and I have some business to discuss."

"Sure," the investigator.

"And maybe I'll see you later," Lenna, with a little smile.

"Sure. In my dreams," the investigator.

On the way back down with Vaca, the investigator, "What kind of business?"

"You mean with Golden?"

"Are they in together?"

Vaca shrugged. "Ask her. If it's her."

"What do you mean if?"

"She has an identical twin," Vaca.

"Identical?"

"I mean really identical. Lena. To where you're not sure who you're in bed with."

"For that you don't need twins," the investigator. "This is a different route?"

"We're going to a restaurant in Denver," Vaca.

"All the way to Denver?"

"I'm hungry."

The investigator was tired, eyes grainy muscles tensing up. But, it was a job.

A parking lot pretty full for ten o'clock Monday night at Pepe's Beer Garden, German-Chinese-Cuban-American Cooking. Inside a magic markered cardboard sign declaring, WELCOME PIG VETS. The clientele was mostly fat middle aged blonds in short sequined skirts dancing polkas and country music with stiff guys who had the bearing of old soldiers fading away. On a stage a band wearing lederhosen included a tuba and accordion. A bar lined with German beer mugs and the tables were heaped with pork and sauerkraut.

"What is this?" the investigator.

"Vets stationed in Germany, married there. Their hangout."

"Pig Vets means they survived the cuisine?"

"Bay of Pigs," Vaca. "Guy giving a talk."

"Okay, why are we here?"

"Got to talk to someone."

A Valkyrian waitress came over. "Hi. Our special tonight is Rocky Mountain Oysters."

"Want to split some bull balls?" Vaca.

"How are they cooked?"

"Who says they're cooked? An order of Oysters and a couple of Weisses."

"Coming up."

"Good for your hormones," Vaca.

The band finished a set and the tuba player came to their table along with the Rocky Mountain Oysters. His hormones looked like he ate them frequently, six feet of broad, blond, heavy muscled, big bellied, lederhosed delicatessen.

"Here for the talk?" the tuba.

"What's it about?" Vaca.

"Probably how the U.S. sold out the anti-Castro patriots. What else is new?"

"Who they got coming?" Vaca.

"Spic patriot survivors. Over at the bar."

They did sort of taste like fried oysters the investigator noticed.

"They cut the guy's balls off," Vaca. "Before they shot him."

"It's more than a simple drug murder. The Colonel was here earlier. It's a warning," the tuba.

"What more? Who to?" Vaca.

"Whoever."

"What's his game, Dee? The Colonel?" the investigator.

"Latin America," Dee.

"Are my cows a warning?"

"Maybe more like a suggestion probably," Dee.

"Suppose I don't want to get mixed up in anything," Vaca.

"Too late. Guys like you you don't want to get mixed up. You're all mixed up."

"Like shit."

"Suit yourself," Dee.

"One thing. Knowing ain't a crime."

"It's not innocent either."

"Knowing what?" the investigator, nobody answered.

Vaca got up, "Ciao muchacho." The investigator followed him out.

"Thought you were hungry," the investigator. In the truck.

"Balls fill you up."

"Knowing what?" The investigator.

Vaca made a sound something like 'a-a-h-r' and stepped on the gas hard. The truck peeled out onto the avenue. "You don't want to know."

The highway back to Boulder, a rental truck cut into lane in front Vaca had to brake abruptly, skidding, a few minutes later the truck cut in so close Vaca went sliding off on the shoulder fighting the wheel, stopped, "I think somebody's telling us something."

Got back on the road soon the rental truck pulled out from the shoulder trailing them. Suddenly huge flakes slapping the windshield like wings. Vaca cursed and put the wipers on high. Soon the glass was turning opaque at the end of each wiper swipe with a strobed vision of the road flapping black white black white black white.

"This is the way weather happens in Colorado," Vaca. "Sudden. This is sudden country. Well, into the blizzard's gizzards."

Cars were spinning off, headlights short funnels of streaming white. Vaca slowed twenty-five, twenty, fifteen.

"No fighting a white-out, I'm pulling off," Vaca, just as they broke through to complete clarity, the white gone like a lifted curtain.

"Guess there's no choice," Vaca.

"What's that?"

"Take the bull by the horns," Vaca.

"What bull?"

"That's the trouble, there's lots of bulls around here. I know, I used to ride em."

"What are we talking about?" the investigator.

"Drugs for sure. Drugs for guns maybe. Possibly guns for something else, I don't know. It's all got to do with the cows but what, is the question. What kind a bull am I dealing with here? What kind of ride we're dealing with depends on the kind of bull. But it's all behind a white curtain."

"You rode them at the rodeo?" the investigator. "Lavigne was telling me about the Denver stock show."

"Professor Lavigne? Oh yeah."

"You know him?" the investigator.

"Oh yeah. A flunky of the guy who runs this conference. I think he's in it for the pussy. I think they both are."

"Lavigne?"

"Oh yeah. He's sorta famous around here. Been seen barking at co-eds walking across campus. Howling even."

"I know how he feels," the investigator. "Especially in spring."

Back in his room at the Boulderado, eye fatigue, prostate kicking up, stomach like he'd been eating acid. Or bull balls. Channel surfing two westerns looking forward to some rest when the phone rang. "There's a Miss Lenna for you."

She was in the lobby, he told her to come up to the room.

Lenna now in packed jeans, loose t-shirt and fleece lined denim jacket was looking just a little dishevelled but it softened the edges. He liked it better that way.

She looked around. "Renovation has improved things a bit."

"To what do I owe?" the investigator.

"It's a habit. I used to come up here to visit Gregory."

"Who?"

"Corso. The Beatnik?"

"I know all about it, I teach it. What was he doing here?"

"They were all here. Burroughs, Ginsberg, Burroughs' son, Anne Waldman. This used to be Chelsea Hotel West."

Or maybe, it suddenly occurred to him, maybe it wasn't softened edges, maybe it was the other one. The twin. Because Lenna's style wasn't poet moll.

But, what the hell. "Talking skin trade with Golden up there?"

She looked blank, then, "Todd. Yes, we . . ."

"So why are you here?"

"I just passed my AIDS test. I'm celebrating."

"Seriously," the investigator. "Vaca says you have the mind of a Ph.D. and the life style of a run-away. What does that mean?"

"Ask him. I brought you a present," pulling a small Chinese looking red box out of her bag.

"What's this?" undoing a latch. Inside two silver ping-pong balls, but heavy as he picked them out making a chiming sound.

"Every man needs a pair of healthy balls," Lenna. "Read the flyer."

"'The Healthy Balls has been handed down up to now and known as Dould Ball of Roaring Dragon and Singing Phoenix.' What? What is this, code?"

"Do I need to decode?" Lenna.

"Show. What you do with balls."

"You roll them around in your hand." She took them and did, they chimed. "It has beneficial effects, especially for tension. I think you're tense."

"Who wouldn't be?"

"Did you know Vaca's land is cursed? It's haunted by the ghost of Chief Left Hand. That could be the answer to a lot of things."

"Like?"

"Go figure," Lenna.

"I hear you have a sister."

"Yes, but she's more interested in the arts. She has the right brain I have the left brain."

"I thought you were more interested in poets."

"But not poetry," Lenna. "Besides, sometimes we switch."

"That's interesting."

"It is odd. It's like moving from Vishnu to Shiva," Lenna.

"Like . . .?"

"They're Hindu Gods."

"We don't have those in New York."

"Sure you do."

"Oh?"

"Creation and destruction. Repetition or change. That's everywhere. Singing Phoenix and Roaring Dragon," Lenna. "Monogamy or variety for example."

"Which are you?"

"Both," Lenna.

"Like me and Golden?"

"Maybe."

"The same night?" the investigator.

Her smile was a blank check. He flashed on the word "dissolute."

His hand floated to her cheek. Her immobility was a license as he caressed her face and then so long, his other hand between her legs. Her body was a grope of complex systems, quivering geometries couched in subliminal fractals. Strong.

"You a jock?" the investigator as they fell into bed.

"Running, skiing, rock climbing. Working out."

"Where are your muscles?"

"Hid by hormones."

She was super wet, he kept wondering about Golden, a certain smell. It was quick for both of them, the Phoenix sang, the Dragon roared. Quick but good. She was a good ball handler, she felt like silk.

He opened his eyes. "You're a Hindu?"

"I have a master."

"Who?"

"He's dead," Lenna.

"Like Jesus."

"But I knew him when he was alive," Lenna. "You're left-handed."

"So?"

"My master was left-handed. And I board my horse up near Left Hand Canyon. Just north of town. You believe in synchronicity?"

"What's to believe?" the investigator.

"For example, three deaths in the mountains connected with Vaca plus his cows dying? Just coincidence?"

"What did the first one have to do with Vaca?"

"Leonard's friend. He wanted to use Vaca's land for an air strip," Lenna. "I'm trying to tell you something."

"Wait a minute. I thought Leonard . . ."

"Right. Now it's up to Leonard. He owes them."

"Who?" the investigator.

"Who usually needs clandestine air strips?" Lenna.

"And what do you have to do with it?"

"I climb with Leonard. Technical," Lenna.

"Whose side are you on?"

"Yours."

"Right," the investigator. "And whose side am I on?"

"Vaca hired you."

"That sure was synchronicity. What other coincidences?"

"You're the investigator," Lenna, "you figure it out."

"I figure you're fucking Leonard. Not to be nosy."

"That's totally coincidental," Lenna.

"To what?"

"To being in the same sleeping bag together at the same time," Lenna.

"What's the coincidence?"

"In the mountains. You get cold. I'm getting cold now."

"Sorry," embracing her from behind, her chilly butt against his dick, but it wasn't long before it was so long again. This time it was longer. And not chatty afterward, the next thing they knew the phone was ringing.

Vaca, without who or hello, "Is Lena up there?"

"I don't know," the investigator.

"What do you mean you don't know?"

"Well one of them is."

"I'd like you to get over to my shop."

"Now?"

"She can drop you," Vaca. "We need your help."

"At what?"

"Leonard's seen a ghost," Vaca.

"A what?"

"A shape shifter."

"A what?"

"A ky-oat. I'll tell you when you get here."

When he got there he found Vaca with Leonard looking like he'd just been fished near drowning out of the surf, and the words 'cold turkey' came to mind.

"I don't believe in this stuff," Leonard.

"Who ever told you you have to believe what you see?" Vaca.

"What did you see?"

"Tell him what you saw, Leonard."

"I was out at Jim's ranch tonight, I thought Jim was there, looking out toward the stable. First there was this globe of greenish-white light sort of bouncing toward me. Then it turned out what I was seeing was a running coyote, but luminous, so that when its feet balled up together it looked like a bouncing globe. But then, that's not what it really was because it turned out to be what looked like an Indian chief riding a pony. Then I got in the car and got the hell out of there."

"That'd be Chief Left Hand," Vaca.

"One hallucination can hide another," the investigator.

"Maybe Leonard's got the D.T.s," Vaca. "Or whatever you get from drugs."

"Protoplasm," Leonard.

"What?" Vaca.

"Those critters weren't made of protoplasm. The way I like it, if it's flesh it's made of protoplasm. Otherwise I get rattled."

"Well we wouldn't want you to get rattled, Leonard. But there's some rattlers around got me rattled and I think we got to do some talking," Vaca.

"If it's not protoplasm it's not friendly," Leonard.

"All right Leonard," Vaca. "It's just Chief Left Hand."

"Maybe he's your problem," Leonard, "scaring your cows to death."

"Other day before dawn there's this steer," Vaca, "just careening around like it was super high, next thing I know it dropped dead."

"Maybe you got a special strain of mile high cow," Leonard, attempting a laugh that came out a croak.

"Think about what you really saw," the investigator. "It's what you don't see that kills you, Leonard. Or comes back to haunt you."

"And what was it he didn't see?"

"An air plane? A helicopter?" the investigator.

"Suppose I let them use it, what then? I'd just be stuck with them," Vaca.

"They'll pay," Leonard.

"I don't need that kind of money."

"Then I'm dead," Leonard.

Vaca shrugged. "Let's all get some sleep."

In the truck, the investigator. "Looks like you have a situation here, so what are you going to do?"

"Do. I ain't doing jack. Ask me in the morning."

In the morning the investigator's phone rang at six-thirty, it was Vaca waiting to have breakfast with him downstairs.

"Ciao muchacho," Vaca.

"How do you get up so early?" the investigator. He was groggy and his prostate recalled last night's fun. He was not used to this kind of schedule.

"I set the radio-alarm to the dog bark station."

"The . . .?"

"Here in Colorado we have a station that broadcasts nothing but dog barks all day. Different ones, so it don't get boring. For people who just want a little company, we prefer it to the talk shows."

"Oh."

"So, did you tie her up and fuck her last night?"

"Is that what she likes?" the investigator.

"Lassoing her and trussing her up like a cow for branding, is what she liked best."

"Well that's not what we did and she seemed to like it okay. So which one does that make her?"

"In that case, it wasn't probably neither of them," Vaca.

"What do you make of Leonard?"

"I don't know. Maybe he's drilling for water. Or maybe he thinks he's going to strike oil."

"Drilling for water?"

"Like the preachers do," Vaca. "Playing your sympathies. Jerking tears. Or maybe just jerking me around."

"Or maybe just jerking off?"

"I don't think so," Vaca. "He's running scared but I don't know if it's away from something or after something."

Trench Fenster came to the table behind the waitress and eggs, "There's not much time," as he sat down.

"I never thought there was," Vaca.

"Better get on it then."

"That can of plutonium still vibrating?" the investigator.

"Who cares, they got twelve point nine tons of the stuff up there."

"How do you happen to know that?" the investigator.

"Enough to kill everyone in the world. Twice." To Vaca, "They're here."

"How do you know?" Vaca.

"The Colonel," Trench.

"From?"

"Colombia and Argentina."

"Who?" the investigator.

"Tourists," Trench. "To ski the Divide."

"With no snow?" the investigator.

"Snow in the mountains, plenty," Trench. "Is he coming?"

"Long's he's still working for me. Where?"

"Up past Charlie Eagle Plume's."

Trench had a big four wheel drive RUV, oversize tires jacked the whole thing up to where it looked like a practical joke. They drove north out of town along the periphery of the high country shelving down to the plains like a beach down to an ocean and panning east across wavy flatness to the sun, a low yolk oozing into the blue monotone, nobody talking much. By now the investigator knew he wasn't going to get anywhere by asking, but Vaca was paying the bills. So why did he feel uneasy? He wasn't a political prude but he did like to know what kind of swine he was getting involved with.

After a while, "They say he was key in importing ex-Nazis to America for intelligence work," Trench.

"Who, Lobe?" Vaca.

"And that now he's disillusioned."

"I wonder why. You believe what he says?" Vaca.

"Lobe? Yeah," Trench. He was wearing dark glasses under his cowboy hat against the brutal light.

"How come?"

"Because he's dying. Cancer."

"How does my expertise get useful in all this?" the investigator, it had been bothering him for some time.

"It doesn't," Vaca.

"Then why am I here?"

"I need a witness," Vaca.

"For?"

"Protection."

"Who protects the witness?" the investigator.

Through a ramshackle town west up into a winding canyon, high red walls shadowing a splashy stream. Vaca dug into his pocket and pulled out an old package of Rolaids, offering them to the investigator, "For altitude sickness."

"I'm not sick," the investigator.

"No, but chew a few of these and you won't be either," Vaca. "Mountain man medicine, we always carry them for greenhorns."

"Well, if it works . . ."

"It's either these or mouse milk and I'm out of mouse milk."

"What's Lavigne's deal?" Trench.

"He's a professor," Vaca. "You could say he sells intelligence. And he consults."

"For who?"

"Whoever pays."

But when they got there there was no one home. There was only one entrance to the place, over a ramp leading to a white spheroid on pylons the cliff falling away below.

"Great view of the Divide," Trench. "They say he built it there to max security."

"Did he build it or did it land?" Vaca.

An old man limped out of the pine woods behind them carrying a large dead dog. Lobe. Probably not as old a guy as he looked but completely bald.

"This is how the Cold War fades away," Lobe. "A dying warrior and his poisoned dog."

"Who did it?" Trench.

"I'd like to say some of your mercenaries but it seems we were all mercenaries. Geopolitics, it looked like a good idea at the time. Something you could assassinate your mother in the name of. But it was just turf then and it's just turf now."

He carried the dog over the ramp and set it down to unlock the door. Then he dragged it in.

"They believe I'm still working for the Company," Lobe. "And to tell the truth it gets so complicated you can't always know. Who are the cowboys and who are the Indians. Or rather who is what when."

"What's the game here?" Vaca.

"Money is always the game. Which means that drugs are always part of it. Did you know that more money is spent world-wide each year for drugs than for food, that's something it's always worth keeping in mind. But there's something else in this case."

"What?" Vaca.

"I'm not sure," Lobe. "Maybe we'll find out when they get here."

They drove up in a Land Rover, five of them, one stocky Israeli with a crazed look in his eye, two Hispanics, one of them very wired, two tall American slabs in dark business suits oozing cynicism and contempt. Nobody was introduced.

"We're here not for trouble," the Israeli. "Just needing information. They couldn't speak English," pointing to the Hispanics, "they brought me along I should interpret. These other guys," the two slabs, "you couldn't understand what they would be saying."

"What do they want?" Vaca.

"They're recruiting. So they are needing a base for a few quick in and outs in certain foreign countries it don't matter which. They're bidding on a contract."

"What kind of contract?" Vaca.

"Maybe you wouldn't want to know. I don't."

Sudden jabbering in Spanish. The Israeli, "They want to open a store here. It's part of a chain."

"Selling what?" Vaca.

"They're not sure yet. Native crafts."

"What natives?"

"Any natives. And maybe New Age chatchkas. But there's a slight problem."

"Transportation," Vaca.

"Right."

Spanish jabber.

"And they also want to buy cows," the Israeli.

"How about car restoration businesses?" Vaca.

"Why not?"

"And what about things like police and laws?" the investigator.

"These two are working for the U.S. government," waving toward the slabs. "It would be a patriotic duty."

"What do they do for the Feds?" Trench.

"We work for Rocky Flats," a slab. "Security."

"Basically, name a price," the Israeli.

"And if I don't?" Vaca.

"This wouldn't be acceptable."

"I need time to think it over."

"Time you got. You got at least twelve hours. No problema. Maybe twenty-four if there's a reason. No hurry."

The wired Hispanic jabbered something to the non-wired Hispanic. Then they all left. No hellos no good-byes.

"You didn't have to kill the dog," Lobe as they walked out.

"So what do you think?" Vaca.

"They're serious," Lobe. "Something more than drugs or besides drugs. Politics, laundering, Rocky Flats. Or all three."

"Why the Flats?" the investigator.

"A lot of people want plutonium," Lobe.

"What are my options?" Vaca.

"Leave town."

"That's it?"

"No. You could leave the state. Or leave the country."

"There are other flat cow pastures," Vaca.

"Not with your rep fronting them," Lobe. "Golden would need that."

"Why?" the investigator.

"You believe in coincidence? Golden used to live down near the JonBenet house when his infant daughter disappeared. Several years ago. The theory was it was a botched kidnapping. A few years later they found her body in the foot hills, signs she had been molested and then eaten. They said coyotes, but there were rumors. Especially when Golden's wife left him. Then she committed suicide. What's that myth about the Greek god who ate his children? Anyway, that's when he moved up to the mountains."

"Did she still have her ears and tongue?" Trench.

Lobe didn't answer.

"Sorry about the dog," Vaca.

"Yeah," Lobe, "me too."

In the RUV the investigator: "What now?"

"Ward."

"Who's that?"

"It's a town," Vaca.

Along the east side of the Divide at nine thousand feet, snowpeaks lining the horizon close enough to see blowing snow. To a town down in a hollow that seemed to be made of rusting metal and spare parts. Stopped in front of a shacky house, Vaca jumped out to bang on the door. La-vigne opened it.

"Why are you here?" Vaca.

"Exactly. I didn't expect to be here. I got a call asking me to come up. I don't know why."

"From who?"

"I don't know who." By then they were all in the house, a one room miner's cabin, a few half broken chairs, a rick-ety table, an unmade bed.

"You always come when called?" Vaca.

"Fellow said Lenna had something to tell me," Lavigne. "I figure that could be something I'd want to hear."

At which point Lenna walked in. Or Lena. Looking sur-prised.

"We having a party?" Lenna. Or Lena.

"You tell us," Vaca.

"Childers called me," Lenna. Or Lena. "He said Leonard had something to tell me about finding the key. About the JonBenet case being symptomatic. I asked him to get Sid Lavigne here because I didn't want to meet him alone. So it looks like everyone's here but Leonard."

"This here's Quonset's shack," Vaca. "He tipped me to this meeting."

"Who's Quonset?" the investigator.

"Dee Quonset. Tubby the Tuba."

"My sister says this man Quonset works for the CIA," Lenna. Or Lena.

Lavigne put his finger to his lips. "He works for something. We're not sure what."

"Just like we're not sure if you're Lenna or Lena," the investigator.

"She's Lena," Lavigne.

"I'm Lenna."

Vaca laughed. "Well, she's Lenna or Lena. And I'm a fox or a chicken. How long we gonna wait around for Leonard?"

"Leonard says Quonset told him they need Vaca's place to store fertilizer," Lenna or Lena.

"Why do they want fertilizer if they're not farming?" Lavigne.

"That's a very interesting question," Vaca. "Trench?"

"Why would I know?" Trench.

"Because they used fertilizer for the big bang in okay city," Vaca. "In Denver the prosecution is trying to connect that with the guys who killed that talk show host."

"The Order?" Trench.

"Aren't you on the same paint ball team as some of those guys?" Vaca.

"I got to take off," Trench. He took off.

Lavigne got a cell phone from his car, started dialing numbers. No answer, they waited a good hour till they heard a loud THUNK! on the wooden shack wall. Rushed outside to find a red splash on the door.

"Injuns?" Lavigne.

"Paint ball," Vaca.

"Maybe somebody's inviting us to leave," Vaca.

"Why do I feel we're being watched?" the investigator. Nobody answered.

The investigator caught a ride down the mountains with Lenna or Lena. He kept trying to figure out whether this was the woman he made love with. She didn't raise the question. Presumably she knew.

"Your talk is this afternoon at four," she reminded him.

In fact he'd forgotten, but he didn't mention that. He just said he wasn't planning anything too elaborate and she said it would be real informal. "And we'll take you out to dinner."

"We? You and your sister?"

"My sister won't be there."

She dropped him at the hotel where there was a message from Todd Golden. He'd forgotten who Todd Golden was then remembered he was the host of the party up in the mountains the night before. Which seemed like weeks ago. He called Golden and met him for coffee at a cafe on the nearby pedestrian mall.

"Leonard," Golden.

"What about him?"

"Nobody's seen him, nobody knows where he is."

"So?"

"Who sent you?" Golden.

"Santa Claus."

"Vaca calls you the investigator. What are you investigating?"

"The murders in the Rue Morgue."

"Where?"

"Why don't you just tell me what you really want to know?"

"We already know what you're up to," Golden.

"What am I up to?" the investigator.

"We don't need your people meddling in our way of life."

"What people what way of life?"

"People from New York. And Hollywood. Like that jew-commy talk show host we blew away in Denver. My people have been clearing and developing this territory for more than a century."

"And Hollywood's been generating the hype. So what's the problem?"

"Right now it's Leonard," Golden. "We need to know what he knows. We need to know it in the next twenty-four hours. Tell Vaca." Golden got up and threw a few silver dollars on the table.

"Where do you get those?"

"The West."

Back to the Boulderado for a nap, but Lenna or Lena woke him up early for a quickie. He was about to kick her out and go back to sleep when she unbuttoned her silky blouse and let it frame a quivery upthrust breast as she walked toward him on the bed.

"You get anyone you want, you and your sister," the investigator, beyond figuring who was who. This wasn't going to be good for his prostate.

"Usually."

"Including Golden?"

"We never tell. Either who we are or who they are. Sometimes we lose track ourselves and start squabbling with one another. But not so much since meeting Todd. He's brilliant with people with low self esteem. He taught us not to fight it, just compartmentalize. Your worthless side is always someone else."

"He's the angel behind the skin business?" the investigator.

"He's in a lot of things around here. It's like he's the local lord, he has more self esteem than anyone. There's a town here named after his family. Where they make Coors."

"Did he buy into your pussy too?" the investigator, as she wiggled her slacks and panties off together.

"Don't be vulgar. Besides, Todd made us understand how some women like to be bought. What's wrong with that? You feel like you're worth something. Ow!"

He'd grabbed a buttock. Now he noticed it was black and blue with lash marks.

"What's that?"

"After you're sold you do as you're told," Lenna or Lena.

"And you like it."

"You submit and you like it. It's part of being someone's property. Now stick your cock in my mouth. I want to make you squirm."

He did as he was told. And he squirmed.

The lecture was in a small room at the city library, a glass and metal structure telescoping toward the steel blue sky. Not students from the university, a small group of work-aged men and women not working on this workday afternoon. But a lot of work shirts, jeans and scuffed cowboy boots. Some branch of the upper hipoisie he wasn't used to.

"His writing shows a tremendous spiritual violence," he told them. "And ghosts are the consequence of spiritual violence. One of the interesting things is that Poe was a decisive force in the origins of both the horror story and the detective story, virtually inventing the latter. That means he was able to tap the energies of both the rational and the irrational, the natural and the supernatural. But it also means that he himself must have been torn apart, shall we say schizophrenic?"

A hand went up. "You mean 'The Murders in the Rue Morgue' as opposed to 'The Masque of the Red Death'?" A guy with a greying pony tail and steel rimmed glasses.

"Very good. That is, what we fail to see, what we refuse to understand even after every conscious effort, comes back to haunt us. That's what a ghost is, a ghost is the return of the incomprehensible that won't be denied."

A thirtyish man with long red hair, pocked face and dirty leather vest made some notes.

"Ghosts, demons, terror, finally despair and a longing for death. Ghosts and Poe and how he sensed a fundamental split in the culture that everyone else wanted to repress. The ghosts in Poe are the ghosts of the Indians exterminated in the development of the West, of the slaves imported to run the plantations, of immigrants from everywhere crushed as surplus labor."

"I thought this was supposed to be about literature," a matronly but nice looking woman in jeans, Mexican shirt and Navajo jewelry.

"Can we get back to the subject at hand?" Lenna or Lena.

The man with red hair was making notes.

"Okay. The important thing about Poe. What's important about Poe is the way he expressed the anxieties beneath the free market system itself. Showed the terrified effort to erect a rational system governed by power as an immense ongoing attempt to deny the self-created undertow of brutality, death and the unknown. The horror. On which we float our pleasant, petty lives."

"Are there any questions?" Lenna or Lena intervening.

The audience looked uncomfortable. He wondered if this was supposed to be the People's Republic of Boulder.

"There's coffee and croissants in the other room," said quickly.

Afterward they walked along the pedestrian mall toward a bar in the Boulderado. The investigator looked sideways and caught a glimpse of her looking down at her breasts, loose in a thin white sweater, as if to see what they were doing and how they might strike an observer. He thought a hitman checking over weapons. Watching through plate glass of the bar as the petty hipoisie floated by, "No wonder you didn't get tenure," Lenna or Lena.

"In academe everybody knows it's just talk, nobody cares. Where's the proletariat in this town?"

"What's the proletariat?"

"You're both fucking him," the investigator.

"Lighten up already."

"He's a creep," the investigator.

"We don't have to like him. We just let him fuck us."

"You like power," the investigator.

"Not exactly. Some women like to fuck men they don't like."

"Some women like whoever's on top."

Hostile silence. They watched the New Age drift past. He sipped his Glen Mackchrankie.

"Lavigne told me how you got kicked out for fucking undergraduates. Speaking of fucking," Lenna or Lena.

"Two undergraduates. He was doing the same thing squared. Cubed."

"What saved his neck?"

"What sacrificed mine is the question," the investigator. "All that was standard practice at the time. The fucking Dean was fucking co-eds, she never had a problem."

"Excuse me, what?"

"They were twins."

"Coincidence," Lenna or Lena.

"But not identical. Not same sex."

"A boy and a girl."

"Approximately. They would each go either way."

"Complicated," Lenna or Lena.

"They'd been molested by their father. And he taught them to make love with one another. So I walked into this. By that time they were disillusioned you might say with love in the social arena. They were making love exclusively with one another. It couldn't last. But it seemed safe to them at least. They were damaged, no question, in the direction of solipsism. I was the freedom father as opposed to the authority father. Who he was was a General in the Strategic Air Command. You know, they were supposed to drop the nukes. He worked in Arapahoe Mountain, not far from here, on and off, that hollowed out mountain they used for Headquarters near Colorado Springs. The fate of the world at their finger tips. How about that. The pressure. Speaking of power. The kids were always followed by security people. If one of them was making out in a car up some lover's lane a mysterious person in a grey suit would lean through the window and say something like, We've told you to avoid exposure in places like this, whereupon the partner would freak and split fast. I tried to convince them it wasn't healthy to screw only one another. Their answer was to cut me in, so the regular thing was the three of us. It was nice. I loved them in a way. I don't say it was therapeutic but at least it was you might say good clean fun. Comparatively.

"The problem was the General found out. He was outraged. Righteous. Accused me of immorality, molestation, pedophilia, double statutory rape, Mann Act violation for crossing state lines with illegal intent though these kids

were no longer minors you understand, also sodomy, fella-
tio, masturbation, pederasty, decadence, corruption, turpi-
tude, professional malfeasance, glandular abnormality,
satyriasis, exploitation of innocence, perversion, mental
disturbance, sexual psychosis, spiritual depravity, violation of in loco parentis, and being from New York. He was
jealous. All this was on the phone and though he was
threatening to shoot me unless I married them, he was be-
side himself, I didn't think any of it was too serious until I
said the word incest and I knew immediately it was a mistake. Power depends on systematic ignorance of certain
subjects. There was a long silence, then he hung up. I realized he had to do something and he did. What he did was
drugs, I never used them, certainly not with the kids, but it
was a cinch for his security people to plant them and alert
the local cops. So that was it, goodbye. The kids left school
shortly afterward, she became bulemic and later I heard
they enlisted in the navy. The General got involved in counter-intelligence in Thailand where he was caught as they
say red-handed in a drug smuggling scheme which led to
implication in a child prostitution ring and either blew, or
had his brains blown, out. The latter I discovered talking to
your friend Childers at Golden's party who by coincidence
knew him through the Colonel in South East Asia. But that's
not all. It turns out that one of the kids, the boy, after fin-
ishing his hitch in the navy, came to Boulder to study Childers didn't know what, and may still be here. They were
sweet kids, there was a sense of terrible pathos about
them, the way they clung to one another, they were only a

little younger than I was, I was twenty-four at the time and I was probably pretty pathetic myself though not pathogenic as I now guess they probably were. I'd like to know what happened to them. Anyway I finished my doctorate but the story has followed me around in the profession."

"Yossi Gottfried," Lenna or Lena. The investigator looked up and realized it was an introduction.

"We've already met," the investigator. He didn't like this guy, the Israeli, there was something crazy in his eyes.

"They found Leonard," Gottfried. "His ears, tongue and genitals missing. Like a cattle mutilation."

The investigator gagged on a mouthful of blue corn chips, washed them down with his microbrew beer.

"This doesn't change anything." Gottfried stalking away.

At dinner Lenna or Lena explained that it was not she but her sister who was involved in the skin business. "Though I've been involved in the skin trade, you could say. At one phase of my life I was making skin flicks. Soft, not hard. Not too hard. I hope you won't hold it against me."

"Hold what against you?" the investigator. "And for how long?"

"I was producing them not acting in them."

"Oh."

"You sound disappointed. I was acting in them a little. The idea was porn films by women. Not exploitative. And genuinely sexy, not just meat market stuff."

"I guess you're a vegetarian?" They were eating in fact in a vegetarian restaurant. The investigator was trying to eat his way through a soy bean cutlet. Every bite seemed to sink immediately to the bottom of his stomach and stay there.

"Can I see one?" the investigator.

"One what?"

"Skin flick. I'm a connoisseur. We have a group, we trade them. We're developing a pornographic hall of fame. Strictly curatorial interest."

"It's been a long time since I did that," Lenna or Lena.

"What do you do now?"

"I fuck poets."

"What about novelists, I tried writing a novel once."

"Only poets. An occasional painter."

"I used to write poetry in creative writing. Does that count? I mean I fuck your sister so what's the difference?"

"I don't exclude ordinary citizens," Lenna or Lena.

"What do you get out of it?"

"I free lance. Culture articles. It's a kind of research."

"Who killed Leonard?" the investigator.

"Golden, obviously. He was looking all over for him. I mean not him he probably paid for it. Or maybe these Latin Americans who are around all of a sudden. Or maybe it wasn't any of those, maybe it was whoever does the cattle mutilations."

"Who does them?" the investigator.

"They say it's the Feds. Can you believe that? I can't."

"Maybe it's another way of putting the pressure on Vaca."

"Vaca can take care of himself," Lenna or Lena. "Leonard was a scum, I don't know what Vaca saw in him, but it's a horrible way to go. I wonder if they just left him to bleed to death."

Pushed her plate, continuing, "I suppose I can tell you now. I swore never to repeat what he told me but what's the difference now? It was Leonard himself who killed his friend in the mountains. The friend had cheated on a drug deal or something. Anyway, Leonard was offered the choice of killing him or being killed himself. They went out for a hike in the mountains, the friend of course had no idea of what was going on, Leonard got him at the edge of a cliff and said he could jump, get shot or take an overdose and tossed him a syringe he'd prepared. The guy thought he was kidding at first. Leonard had a gun on him, found a long stick or something and started prodding him, the friend held on to the stick but lost his balance. Leonard let go and he went over. When he checked at the bottom the friend was still alive so he shot him up with the syringe and he went out like a light. Then Leonard came down to my place and told me he was going to commit suicide, he still had the gun. I told him I didn't want blood all over my house and he couldn't bring his friend back anyway. So he calmed down a little, but from then on he wasn't really himself, if he ever was, I mean that was part of the trouble that Leonard didn't know who he was and anyway I think he really wasn't anybody, a non-entity so far as I could see, nothing inside."

"Maybe a lot of us are like that," the investigator.

"Maybe a lot of us are like that. Maybe all of us are like that. I know something about it as a twin, when you know you could just as well be one person as another, depending on the circumstances."

"Or that anybody can do anything, depending on the circumstances, that people don't necessarily act in character, as they say, which makes you suspect there is no such thing as character, that personality is just a place of passage for mysterious forces."

"Anyway," Lenna or Lena. "You're getting too deep for me. All I can tell you is that's when Leonard started having hallucinations."

Vaca picked him up at the hotel later that night and told him they were going to see Childers. "I wanted you to be in on this." When they got there, a nice suburban ranch house with a big lawn, Tubby the Tuba was pulling up on a motor cycle.

"We have a situation here," Childers.

"Tell me about it!" Vaca.

"I know you're on the spot," Childers. "You want my advice? Okay, and remember this is only advice, take it or leave it, but let me say I've been in touch with, let's just say, people. Just do this one shot. Dee here," nodding to Tubby the Tuba, "will go along. Dee Quonset? After that it won't be your business anymore."

"It's not my business now," Vaca.

"I beg to differ. Unfortunately for you," Childers.

"What choices do I have?" Vaca.

"That's your choices."

"I want him along, the investigator."

"All right. But you better start. And leave the motor cycle here, they make too much noise."

When they got up to Vaca's spread it was well dark but there was a full moon casting a gauze of silvery light, the peaks of the Divide glittering on the horizon. Before very long a motor snarling from the south. It circled once snapped on some super-bright landing lights and made its approach. Touching down bounced along the field like Leonard's version of Chief Left Hand's ghost and when it stopped a rental truck appeared from somewhere and pulled alongside. It was a small single engined Cessna. The investigator still wasn't sure why he was there but he assumed it was to help keep Vaca out of trouble. When they got to the plane they saw it was packed solid with bales of money, hundred dollar bills stacked and tied with plastic bands like newspapers just off the press. The investigator was stunned. Then he was angry.

"I don't want to be mixed up in this," the investigator. "You should have warned me."

"Take it easy. We're working for the Feds here," Vaca.

The pilot, skinny, ratty hair, severe five o'clock shadow, looked like living road kill, he waved at the rental truck. Two Asians jumped out, one short and fat the other tall and cadaverous.

"These are Feds?" the investigator.

Each Oriental pulled a pitch fork from the truck and began bailing stacks of dollars from the plane into the truck. Nobody talked. When Vaca asked the two Orientals something they jabberred at him in Oriental. The pilot was super-nervous, crazed gaze, the investigator guessed amphet-amine.

The Orientals worked fast but not fast enough for the pilot who kept looking behind him seeing enemies behind cottonwoods. After a while the pilot: "I wish they'd hurry up. I'm going to miss my Shiatsu appointment in Aspen. This guy looks like a pig," pointing at the investigator, "who brought him along?"

"I did," Vaca.

"I don't like him."

"Maybe I don't like you," the investigator.

"You from back east?" the pilot. "Jew York? Work for a bank, right? Or for the Feds, same thing, banks, Feds, Jews, United Nations, same fucking thing. Too damn smart, out here we shoot faggots like you, take them out like coyotes whenever we oof!" the investigator caught him with a kick to the balls he doubled over straightened up with a gun in his hand Quonset grabbed his wrist twisted till the gun dropped.

"That was a Delancey Street Uppercut, now how about you shut your trash face," the investigator.

"Watch it muchacho," Vaca, "don't get in the way of busi-ness."

When they finished the plane bounced down the field and off, the rental truck headed out, Vaca, Quonset and the investigator drove to Vaca's ranch house, a small cabin made of logs.

"Built it from a kit," Vaca.

They were in a bed room living room arrangement. Quonset went to the phone in the kitchen. When he came back he said they're not happy at the office in Oklahoma City.

"Why not?"

"Who knows what makes them happy or unhappy back East."

"I thought . . ." Vaca.

"Yeah," Quonset. "Talk to Childers."

"So we're in trouble?" the investigator.

"How would we know?" Quonset. "We'll know if we're in trouble when somebody troubles us. Till then we're not in trouble."

For the first time it occurred to the investigator that he was frightened and he simultaneously realized he'd been frightened for a long time. Maybe he'd always been frightened, maybe he'd always been running scared. Of what? Suddenly he was thinking of Lenna. He was atrociously horny and he wanted to get her into the sack again. Or Lena. He wondered if he'd ever get them both in the sack at the same time.

The investigator told Vaca to drop him anywhere in Boulder because he felt like walking but Vaca said he had to meet his wife at the Boulderado anyhow.

"I didn't realize you were married."

"Sure. Lorna."

When the investigator glimpsed Lorna at the Boulderado he thought she looked just like Lenna or Lena. He was surprised and mentioned it to Vaca, who assured him she looked nothing like Lenna or Lena. Maybe not, but she had the same regular facial features, the same athletic but voluptuous build, the same chestnut hair, the same soft way of moving and you could have fooled him.

The investigator was awakened in the morning by a call from Vaca: they'd kidnapped his wife.

"When? How?"

"They just broke in with guns and took her. We were making love, they pulled her out of bed, threw my suit jacket around her and dragged her out half naked." His voice was steady but leaden, he was breathing heavily.

"Did they say why, what they want?"

"They said they'd be in touch, but I guess it's obvious."

"Who were they?" the investigator.

"Remember those two big guys we met in the mountains? The ones who looked like bouncers in business suits? Well it wasn't them but they were just like them. I mean they looked the same but they weren't the same people."

"If they looked the same how could you tell?"

"I don't know, I could just tell," Vaca.

"Like, their voices?"

"No, their voices were the same. Don't nitpick petty details, I'm not in the mood."

"You can't go to the police of course?"

"That wouldn't be smart," Vaca. "I've been talking to Childers on and off all night, I'll fill you in. An hour."

It was obvious he'd been up all night, clothes rumpled, blond five o'clock shadow, red eyes. There was enough whisky on his breath to knock over a horse. "She didn't make a sound when they dragged her out, she was in shock, but she was fighting like a bobcat, the jacket wasn't so much to cover her nakedness as to help keep her arms pinned to her sides but she kept squirming out of it to get at them with her nails, she was scratching and biting and kicking but not a sound."

The investigator didn't answer, there was nothing to say.

"I was moving hard inside her, she was just beginning to come. They just grabbed me and pulled me out, I didn't know what was happening."

They weren't headed for Childers' house the inspector noticed.

"I get this repeated image of how her breasts kept spilling out of my jacket as she was fighting them. She was wriggling and flopping like a trout. And I couldn't do a thing."

"Where are we headed?" the investigator.

"It happened very fast. The weird thing was after I heard their van pull away I realized I still had an erection. Christ."

"Where are we headed?"

"The thing is sex is her weak point. Anybody can make her do anything if they get her excited enough. I can't help it I keep thinking about what happened once they got her in that van, how long did she keep struggling? I been thinking about that all night. What they're doing to her."

"Did they have a license?"

"Licence? You don't get a license to do stuff like that."

"Plate number."

"No it was too dark," Vaca. "It happened so fast it was like a dream. A nightmare. What if I never see her again?"

They were out of town now the mountains on the right, going through a place called Marshall. There wasn't much of it. Pulled up in front of a shacky looking house, "This here's an old miner's cabin," Vaca. "We're on top of a big old coal mine. It was deserted over a hundred years ago because of a fire down there. It's still burning, you can see the smoke coming up in some places."

The cabin was deserted, some bed springs, a bridge chair or three.

"Why are we here?" the investigator.

"You'll see."

After a while a car pulled up and someone knocked. He announced himself as "Doctor Snowt, D.D.," a tall, cadaverous man with greying hair, dark suit, black sport shirt, black fedora, and oily manners who seemed more like an undertaker or from the gold cross he wore around his neck some sort of Christian.

"You were referred to me by Doctor Crow I believe?"

Vaca nodded, "Doctor Crow and Doctor Childers."

"For a consultation?"

Vaca nodded.

"What seems to be the problem?"

"I thought you knew."

Snowt was silent. Then, "You need a replacement."

"A replacement? No, I want the original back."

"Oh. You're the one with the wife. Sorry."

"What's happening to her?" Vaca.

"I can't tell you exactly, but these people usually maintain them in good health. Probably on some harmless drug."

"And then what?" Vaca.

"And then they use them as needed, of course. How old is she?"

"Twenty-seven."

"Well it's more mature than usual, they're usually children, sometimes teens, but you never know when the suitable circumstance will come along."

"What do you mean by use them?" Vaca.

"You raise cattle, don't you? And renovate cars? Well, they're in business too."

"So?"

"Don't worry, I'll speak to Doctor Crow. You may have something they want."

"I do," Vaca.

"Then give it to them."

"Arrange it."

"I assure you I'll do my best. I'm sure it will work out."

On the way back in the car, "What did you think of that?" Vaca.

"Blackmail obviously," the investigator. "And something else. Do you really want to hear this?"

Vaca nodded.

"Some kind of forced prostitution ring. I know it's crazy. Maybe they send them to Latin America."

Vaca didn't say anything.

The investigator had a lunch appointment with Lavigne first they took a walk in the near mountains overlooking the town, the plains, from certain places you could see the skyscrapers in Denver like a toy town in the distance. Lavigne, talking about Vaca, "He hasn't been the same since his affair with Lenna or Lena, I don't remember which one he said it was. She walked out on him for Golden, Vaca thought it was for his money but it wasn't. It was for his power, that's what she likes. Anyway, that's my opinion but I don't know that much about either of them."

"Recently?"

"Yeah, not long ago."

"How did his wife take all this?"

"Wife?" Lavigne. "What wife?"

Just then a perspective opened up to the south and Lavigne indicated a distant complex of miniscule metallic buildings and structures on a plateau, not obvious unless pointed out. "That's what all the fuss is about, Rocky Flats."

"It's closed now isn't it?" the investigator.

"That's what they say but can you believe anything they say? Besides they still got all that shit over there. Too close for comfort. And there are these renegade cowboys and housewives on the former grand jury who want to open up the secret report on what's really going on there."

"What do you think is really going on?"

"Genetic alteration probably, mutation from excess radiation, theft of plutonium for third world A-bombs, irradiated food processing experiments, environmental calculation of exposure levels, contamination of water supplies, cattle mutilation, manufacture of replacement human flesh, growing human sperm in mouse testes, banking frozen embryos, producing clone your own spare part twins, strange albino crossbred mammals, contact with aliens via radioactive frequencies, what do I know? It's basically Doctor Frankenstein over there. If not Doctor Faust. Not that I'm a Luddite. I believe in progress, don't you? Doctor Frankenstein is not Doctor Mengele."

"The rumor is that Doctor Mengele moved to the New World along with Werner von Braun, but set up shop in Latin America."

"Anyway, they got tons and tons of that shit over there," Lavigne, "they've got to do something with it."

In the car back to town the investigator aware of a smell he thought from the upholstery but now realized was emanating from Lavigne, a strange combination of perfume and decay. At lunch Lavigne treated him to a boring discourse on his philosophy of self-promotion as a personal branch of the free market with the self as commodity, everything for sale. Lavigne was doing well, a tenured professor plus steady employment on a consulting basis thanks to his connections with the liberal wing of the spy establishment, he let on, what he did exactly, of course, he wouldn't say, but he let on. And he believed in it. "The intelligence community isn't all bad. There are factions. I mean who would you rather have do it, me or some off the wall right winger? Besides, what would we do without intelligence?"

Also, he loved to let on to young women, out of whom the hell was impressed, he confided. One of them, Ella, sat down at the table for a while, a waitress where they were eating, he suspected that's why Lavigne took him there. A man with red hair and leather vest signaled from the next table she got up he murmured something to her.

"She looks like a sophomore," the investigator.

"She just graduated. Fair game. I'm going skiing with her later, want to come?"

"In this weather?"

"The weather down here is not the weather up there. And I have a cabin with a small hot tub and a small sauna. Just big enough for three in fact. And I need to stop off to see Lobe on the way."

Ella hurried from table to table waiting, a big girl, klutzy even, but the investigator liked the way she moved, a little like a giraffe. Besides, he wanted to see Lobe.

Sitting in the living room of his house in the mountains, which he called the flying saucer, Lobe was gloomy. He hadn't been feeling very well and he was scheduled to have more chemo, which he loathed. He stared at the white line of the Divide and talked about it.

"They put you in this tiny cubicle plugged into the machinery through your veins. You become an extension of the machine. For hours. And you think, after a while, that this is the normal state of things, you've always been part of the machine only it hasn't been so tangible. The technology and mentality of as they say, late capitalism. You're just so used to it you don't notice. The Japs have a computer program now, they call it Geisha, where you can plug into the prerecorded orgasms of famous actresses and rock stars to stimulate your own. I've killed people, at the beginning I was a field agent and on occasion I had to do it, more than once. Once someone asked me, it was a woman, how can you do something like that? I thought a minute and my answer surprised me. I said, You get used to it. Besides, the organism itself, the human organism, seems less important than it used to. The human race is moving away from the flesh, maybe it's moving away from the human race itself. I have a few more months, maybe a year, before mine withers away, depending on how much I want to plug into the life support technology. Right, the human race is about to have a lobotomy. Another quantum of flesh drops from the tree of life. Another articulation of the genetic code is lost, but the language remains. Everything else is replaceable, interchangeable, expendable, but the language remains."

Ella was gawking at the fantastic house, the view of the Divide, this sort of exotic windbag who admitted to killing people. She didn't talk much, hardly said anything on the drive up, but the investigator could tell she was fascinated, excited, and that Lobe was really feeling her oats. Suddenly he intuited that this monologue was a performance for her, for her heavy breasts, ponderous thighs, swollen lips, that Lobe was vamping her juices, mentally groping, probing for DNA like some kind of giant disgusting mosquito.

Lavigne explained to her, "He's had two lives, a double agent."

"At least," Lobe.

"One in intelligence, the other as a novelist."

"Intelligence and counter-intelligence," Lobe.

"That explains his eloquence," Lavigne, "not one of those popular novelists but genuine high culture, one of the heirs of Proust."

"Prunes?" Ella. Impressed.

"What I wanted to get your reading on," the investigator, "in plain language, is what kind of game Vaca's playing."

"Out here on the plains plain language is never plain."

"Cards on the table."

"Ah. But he never puts his cards on the table. In that sense he's one of the real sons of the Golden West, as they call it, i.e., snake oil drummers, showmen, impresarios, Buffalo Bill turning even Geronimo into a side show. But the old West was always part mirage, part tall story, a medicine show, a projection of business interests and armed mercenaries promoted by the journalists, painters and novelists of the time. Why? The bigger the rip-off the better the odds. This is no secret, there are very few secrets really, what it is is that we're just prevented from thinking about certain things. Like death. We know about them but we don't think about them. We're distracted."

"What do you think about dying?" Lavigne.

"It's like working. It's easier to do it well than to do it badly. You know you're okay if no one is feeling sorry for you."

"I have to show the investigator here some mountain real estate. How about if we leave you Ella for a while. O'kay Ella?"

"Absolutely."

"Be nice," Lavigne. He left with the investigator.

In the car, "What's this about real estate?" the investigator.

"It's clear she's ready to jump into bed with him, you didn't need radar to pick up the signals."

"Interesting," the investigator. "Some people are afraid to be around death."

"Men. Some women are attracted to it, my observation. Death and power. Though he never killed anybody, come on."

"You sure?"

"How could I be sure, I just doubt it. Anyway he's not going to fuck her. Or even if he does that's not the point."

"What is it then?" the investigator.

"Dreams. He gets into people's heads and finds out what their dreams are. He even buys dreams. A kind of reverse psychoanalysis, he pays people by the hour to lay there and narrate their dreams while he takes notes."

"Why does he do this?"

"For his novels, for the stories. But it started as an interrogation technique in the intelligence. Then they used it in propaganda campaigns, so they could find out how they could really get to people. Now it's used in advertising. So you see what they develop in the military often pays off for tax payers in civilian life."

"Where are we going?" the investigator.

"I want to show you something."

A winding dirt road among pines then stopped at an old mine entrance, a small, ramshackle log portal in the side of a steep slope, some sort of slag heap to one side. There was a cabin facing it and a tall, skinny guy with a scraggly beard and striped denim overalls limped out carrying a rifle.

"This here's private," said the beard.

"Lobe sent us," Lavigne.

"You want in?"

Lavigne nodded. The beard limped over to the mine opening using the rifle as a cane and unlocked a metal grill, picked up a big flash light inside the entrance and led them in. The small tunnel quickly widened into a sizable chamber. It was strewn with plastic and metal prostheses of every imaginable sort, most with stray wiring attached, many damaged or in any case unidentifiable as particular body parts.

"What is this?"

"It's a dump," Lavigne. "They think some of it may recycle but in fact they don't know what to do with it all. Too valuable to just trash. Some entrepreneur could start a profitable salvage business in body parts."

"Who dumps here?"

"There are already a couple of specialist electronic prostheses start-ups in town. They use a powerful computer technology that in some instances puts them in direct competition with organ dealers."

"Are we talking music now?"

"Human organs," Lavigne.

"So what's this got to do with me?"

"Vaca. He was helping a friend sell goat glands to society doctors doing experimental impotence surgery. They were working with a pharmaceutical looking for a new aphrodisiac. The pharmaceutical was trying to track down something the Mayans used so they bought a rain forest in Guatemala. Meantime the prosthesis companies got some venture capital and started collaborating on a small electronic device with an ultra thin plastic jack installed in the urethra that could crank up an erection at the press of a button. At that point the conglomerate that owned the pharmaceutical merged with the multinational that owned the venture capital unit, which also happened to own a spin-off called General Prosthetics that constructed all sorts of body replacement parts and was ready to go head to head with the companies that supply human organs to the hospitals for transplants. But then the spin-off was folded in, as I understand, after which everything got too murky for anybody to follow except maybe the accountants."

When they got back to the flying saucer Ella wasn't there.

"Where is she?" the investigator.

"Oh, a friend dropped by and she went back down with him."

"That's ridiculous," Lavigne, "she was going skiing with us at Eldora."

"She remembered something she had to do," Lobe. "Does she have relatives here, a boy friend?"

"Why?"

"Just asking."

Three quick bangs from outside, "What was that?" the investigator.

"Nothing," Lobe.

"Shots?"

"Nothing important, just Gottfried doing target practice. He has a thing with guns."

Yossi came in the front door, no gun in sight. Belligerent, "If you would show some brains, maybe you wouldn't hang around here too long."

"We're saving our brain cells," Lavigne, "we don't want to use them up too fast."

Yossi made two quick moves and had Lavigne in a headlock bent double and helpless. "You sarcastic little pimp. Maybe I could waste all your fucking brain cells with one shot, you would like that? Brain cells are one thing we don't need, they don't keep," he shoved Lavigne away he stumbled against a wall and slumped to the floor.

"Get rid of them," to Lobe, walking out of the room. "Before I do."

In the car in a state of shock, the investigator driving, "What happened?"

Lavigne was feeling his neck as if it hurt. "At the least, he has a bad temper."

For the investigator Yossi's outburst was an articulation of something he'd been sensing all along. What? And what was that remark that brain cells don't keep? Something lost in translation? The investigator felt a sickening uneasiness settling in.

"What was Gottfried doing there?" Lavigne. "And whose side is Lobe on?"

"What are the sides?" The investigator wanted to see Lenna or Lena. He felt on overwhelming need to get laid. He wanted to forget about all this stuff. He remembered that he'd come out here on a sort of vacation, with a little consulting on the side. He'd thought that he was going to tell someone something about ghosts, maybe the sucker stuck with the local haunted house. Instead he was being sucked into something he didn't understand and about which he didn't care. He didn't know what was at stake. He didn't know what the game was or who was playing against who or even who was on what team. He knew he should change his plane ticket and leave tomorrow and he knew he wouldn't. What he didn't know was why he wouldn't.

They stopped in Nederland, a mountain village looked like it had been put there by accident, and walked into a dark timbered bar populated by bearded men in denim and women in pioneer dresses. Ordered a couple of beers.

"These little mountain towns," Lavigne. "People think you find decadence in the big city. What goes on here it's scary. One guy keeping his dead grandpa on blocks of ice. Home spun cryogenics. Figures on thawing him when the science is right. That's the direction of the whole culture. Death as the last frontier."

"So where is she?" the investigator.

"The trouble is, there's a lot of radiation here because of the altitude, because of natural uranium deposits, because of mine tailings, and more from Rocky Flats. And nobody knows how much the organs of a body in suspended animation will sop up."

"Where is she?" the investigator.

"Or even how much living bodies absorb. Humans or even cows. Maybe she did catch a ride down."

They didn't say anything for a while.

"What do we do if she doesn't show up?" the investigator. "Go to the police?"

"And tell them what?"

"Well we can't just do nothing."

"Why can't we? That's what we usually do."

"About what?" the investigator.

"About everything. It's only people like Lobe and Gottfried and the Colonel that actually do something. And they just make it worse."

The investigator thought about it, about not doing anything. The more he thought about it the more he thought it was true. But probably not for the reasons that Lavigne thought it was true. It was more because he didn't know which side he was rooting for any more. It was like not having a home team. He couldn't exactly tell you when this situation began, but he thought it started when he was a little kid and the Brooklyn Dodgers and New York Giants moved to the West Coast. That was a violation of something basic, not merely for New Yorkers but an augury of a new order however as yet mysterious.

Lavigne took him out on a cross country ski track but the investigator wasn't used to the altitude soon they had to quit. In the car snaking down through a red walled canyon playing hide and seek with a leaping creek. A black motorcycle caught up with them, pulled alongside, then tailed their rear bumper, hanging there as if the car were towing it. The man on the motorcycle had no helmet or goggles and bright red hair whipping in the slipstream. He stayed right there till the road flattened out in Boulder, then disappeared in the traffic.

A note from Vaca at the Boulderado to meet at a lawyer's office, a down town address. There was just enough time. The sign on the door said Snowt and Crow, Attorneys. Vaca was in a waiting room thumbing a nature magazine.

"The white rhinocerous, the condor, the panda, the salmon, the rain forests, whales, gorillas, tigers, toads. You see what's happening. Even the elephant." He didn't look too upset about it. There was enough whisky on his breath to kill off an endangered species.

"What's the story?"

"She's safe but they're keeping her."

"Who?" The investigator guessed Vaca was engaged in some charade but couldn't figure why.

"Who is the question."

Snowt wasn't there. They spoke to Crow. Crow was not exactly fat, say stout, full of an easy amiability, the kind of amiability you don't trust. "We've received a fax from someone named Mork, maybe it's a joke. Do you know a Mork?"

"No, what's it say?"

"I gave you the gist on the phone," Crow. "What I didn't tell you was that it came with a P.S. in a code based on the I'Ching which when worked out said 'no harm.' They left an e-mail address and we checked in. I think we can relax a little, it's probably just a matter of time."

"I spent two hours chanting this afternoon," Vaca, "and I think everything's going to be okay. And if it isn't, so what? I guess you didn't know I was a Buddhist. They call me the Karmic Cowboy. Hi-ho Siva!"

The investigator thought he was going to have to help Vaca out of the office, but he made it on his own.

"Well," the investigator, "the message seems like good news anyway."

"Of course it's good news," Vaca. "I wrote it."

He was almost getting fond of Vaca. "And are you really a Buddhist?"

"She's a Buddhist, she's a Nudist, she's whatever is cutest," he sang. "Lorna. We're invited to Golden's for breakfast."

Next morning the investigator drove up to Golden's with Vaca. The investigator had spent the previous night with Lenna or Lena. So had Vaca it turned out. He said.

Trench and Snowt were already there when they arrived, already eating. They were all eating liver, there was a platter of it in the middle of the breakfast table.

"Have some liver," Golden. "We always have liver for breakfast up here, some people like it some don't. You can almost eat it raw, it's good for you. We have a special source. In some tribes they actually eat the raw liver of a defeated enemy, did you know that? There's also oat meal."

The investigator and Vaca opted for oat meal.

"This is about cryogenics," Golden. "You know what that is of course," shlupping a slice of nearly raw liver into his mouth.

"I should know," Vaca. "They froze my great granma."

"What do you mean they froze your grandmother?"

"Great granma. Before my part of the family come up from New Mexico. It's part of the family story. See, when she was dying they knew they couldn't get the family together in time for the funeral because the family tradition was they have to bury someone as soon as they die. I'm not sure where that come from cause all the regular Spanish families in the area would wait till the corpse was the other side of ripe."

The investigator had already noticed that when Vaca started telling a story he lapsed into thick Cowboy, a dialect spoken only by a few oldtimers and everyone in Western movies.

"Yeah, the family had a parcel of peculiar customs, we are part Spanish. But not Chicano, Spanish from the old Conquistadores, or that's the legend, that we been in the area now for five hunerd years," he said hunerd instead of hundred. "Other customs were, like, my granny and grandpa spoke in this secret language nobody else in the family understood, and we used to eat these funny flat crackers now and then that nobody else did or knew what they were. Now part of the family'd already settled up in Dinver," he said Dinver for Denver, "and it would a took them three days to get back down to Taos by stage, there wasn't a railroad yet on that route. Now I don't remember this real well cause I was just a young one but they say that on week ends the old men would wear these funny little black hats. So what they say is they got together with these black hats and started singing songs in this secret language and everything and they got these big cakes of ice, they shipped them down from the high mountains. And see greatgrandma was unconscious anyways so they just lay her out on these cakes of ice and she went into what you call suspended animation. Then by the time the family got there the ice'd melted and she resumed dying in the normal way. So they were able to have a great proper funeral with everybody there."

"You trying to say you're from one of those Jew families that came over here with the Conquistadors after we wiped them out in Spain?" Golden. "I might have known, a troublemaker like you."

"I ain't sayin' I'ma jist tellin'," Vaca's accent was getting thicker by the minute. "An' as to bean a troublemaker, shecks, we cowboys's always been an independent bunch. Sheet, I remember one day when I was doin' the rodeo circuit, my big thing was ridin' the bulls . . ."

"Your big thing is still the bull," Golden. "Let's get down to business."

"Your Mercedes'll be all set in two weeks," Vaca, "the hang up was the factory sent the wrong size pistons plus I had to go the wrecking yard route for some of the body parts, I been picking around car cemeteries like an auto ghoul. You still want that stash box in the ash tray?"

"Yes, but never mind that now."

The Golden boys were all putting away slice after slice of oozy purple pinkish liver, liver juice dribbling their chins.

Snowt poked in, "Dr. Childers tells us that the story about your wife is dubious at best . . ."

"Get a rope," Crow.

"You can drop the doctor crap," Trench.

". . . and at worst is some kind of probe, so I don't know what you think you're doing because you're getting yourself into deep shit . . ."

"We don't care what he's doing," Golden. "What we care about is what he's going to do. Now I'm going to finish up my liver here and leave, and you're going to talk it out with Trench."

Golden shlupped the last of the bloody liver, washed it down with a cup of coffee and ambled out.

"All right, so what the devil is going on here?" Vaca.

"And don't crap around about the devil," Snowt, he pulled a cross from under his shirt.

"Okay," Trench, "there's going to be a shipment from down south and we're going to need special equipment, a semi with refrigerator capability."

"So?" Vaca.

"So, we're just telling you. Plus, and here's the important thing, there's going to be a safari, down to Sao Paolo this time, and it's going to be a big one, we got a big commission down there."

"Who knows about this?" the investigator.

"Shut up," Trench. "What's he doing here? All of which means we're going to need some permanent freezer capability at your place."

"Which I have to build?" Vaca. "He works for me."

Golden reappeared, "I want to show you two something." He led them out into a corridor and suddenly they found themselves in a bath room, Golden lifted the toilet seat, "Take a look in there."

They looked and saw an enormous piece of shit.

"Get a good look," Golden, "I want you to remember that. That's a Golden turd."

In Vaca's truck on the way back down to town, "At least he didn't try and make us eat it," the investigator.

"That'll come," Vaca.

"Childers said it was a one shot deal and you're out," the investigator.

"One shot sure seems to lead to another don't it."

"What are they shipping?"

"Don't even ask," Vaca.

"Suppose Childers doesn't really work for the Feds?"

"I been thinking about that."

"What do you think?" the investigator.

"Then I'd be fucked."

"What's a safari?"

"That's when you go out on a hunt and kill animals and bring back their body parts as trophies."

"You're not really Jewish?"

"Sure gets him hot under the collar, don't it?"

Vaca dropped him off, walking back to the Boulderado the investigator crossed paths with a group of four or five punk people stalking down the mall like a hunting party, green and orange mohawks the men torn t-shirts heavily tattooed with pierced nipples the women ripped jeans pierced ears noses lips navels and god knows what else also tattooed, they could have been a heavy metal band visual noise some new kind of insect life, a moving agglomeration of miscellaneous interchangeable technomutant body parts segmented by chains leather and plastic in odd disintegrations of organicity. Just behind them a pock faced man in motorcycle jacket whose flaming red hair next to the green mohawks also looked dyed.

"Hey!" the redhead. "Don't stare. It's just body language, everyone speaks it."

"Who are you?" the investigator.

"I'm an old beatnik, we still got em out here. Just a link in the chain."

"What's your game?"

"I work for Invisible, Inc. I'm a private dick. Mostly we shadow people. I been shadowing you."

"How long?"

"How Long is my partner."

"You mean his dick?"

"Whose dick?"

"I don't know any Dick, I'm saying how long."

"That's what I'm saying, How Long."

"I don't know how long. How long what?"

"No, just How Long."

"That's impossible. Look, let's start from scratch. You don't know Dick and you don't know how long either?"

"I do know How Long."

"How long?"

"That's what I said."

"I give up," the investigator.

"O'kay, but if you see a tall Chinese looking man behind you don't get excited, he's there to protect you. That's our new assignment. Usually I'm on second shift."

"Who's on first?"

"Never mind, it's not important."

Having brunch. In a creole cookery with Lenna or Lena. Brunch was the kind of thing Lenna or Lena liked, big stacks of food with bloody marys at eleven A.M. everything pumped full of cayenne pepper, the basic idea was excess. The investigator was trying to eat his way through it, belching sweating from red pepper, getting woozy on bloody marys.

"Vaca is married or not?" the investigator.

"He's been talking about his wife again?" Lenna or Lena. "Another one of his tall tales. She died years ago. Raped and murdered, they never caught anybody."

"That's a tough one," the investigator.

"Death is a tough one," her eggs benedict oozing over her lower lip.

"What else is new?"

"Death is the last frontier," slipping a slice of ham into her mouth.

"Well what are we doing about it?"

"Mmmnn," shaking her finger while she finished swallowing. By now they were both streaming with pepper sweat. "We're pioneers. Taking the initiative in all kinds of research. At the Denver hospital they're transplant wizards, skin is just a piece of the pie. The spare parts business is booming, transplants, synthetic organs, fetal grafts, computerized prostheses, genetically altered animal tissue. We're getting to the point where we'll be able to support a given brain indefinitely. Which means consciousness, which is about as close as we can get to immortal."

"What about brain replacement?" the investigator.

"That never. Much as some people need it. They don't keep. Rebuilds someday, maybe."

"And the population problem, since there are already too many . . ."

"No problem. War, famine, plague, genocide, the basic brutality of human nature. It solves itself," Lenna or Lena.

"Self-liquidating," the investigator. "Like the human race."

"We see eye to eye."

"And tooth to tooth."

"Tooth?" Lenna or Lena.

"Fang? Claw? Tennyson? Poetry?"

"Don't get snotty, elitism is down the toilet. What we're doing is actually intervening in nature for the first time ever to alter not only the brain's environment but its host organism too. Do you know what that means? As of now the mind can control the basic conditions of its own existence. Not just talk about it."

"Yeah, well. Banzai. Talking about it can change it too. Always has. Or writing about it."

She didn't even answer, just made like she got a whiff of garbage. Then added, "I like poets, they know how to play. But you don't take that stuff seriously."

"I take it seriously when they take it seriously." He was by now marinating in pepper sweat, the establishment obviously made it a point of honor to test the cayenne macho of its clientele. He went to the men's room to find a towel, took his dick out to piss for good measure when he felt himself pushed violently against the urinal, a catlike oriental voice murmuring, "Not to move."

"How Long?" he guessed.

"Y-e-e-s. How Ling. How short for Howard, he always get wrong."

"Can I finish up here?"

"Y-e-e-s. But not to leave. Is dangerous out there now." Zipping up, "Why dangerous?"

"Y-e-e-s. A Mister Fenster."

"He's a friend of mine."

"Not now. Now dangerous." He looked around, found a window painted over, cracked the frame open with a karate blow. "You go out now."

"But I was with . . ."

"I will tell."

Wriggled out into a back alley rented a car drove to Vaca's garage. He was on the phone so he wrote him a note: 'why is fenster after me?' Vaca looked at it raised his eye brows, wrote back still talking: 'who says he is?' The investigator: 'how ling.' Vaca: 'what howling?' signalling he'd be off in a minute.

Hanging up, "What are you taking about, something's howling at you?"

"You don't know this oriental detective or body guard or whatever, How Ling?"

"Don't know what you're talking about," Vaca.

"And Fenster?"

"If Fenster's after you you got trouble. Sorry. My guess is where I want a witness Golden doesn't want any."

"Great. And this oriental and his redheaded friend?"

"There's a redheaded friend? Don't know anything about it. Something must have activated a third force. Unless Childers . . .?"

"Or Lobe?" the investigator.

Vaca shrugged. "No knowing."

"How's your wife?"

"She's okay now," Vaca.

"So what do I do now, leave town?"

"Maybe. Go see Childers first, ask him about a third force."

It was after nightfall, Childers asked the investigator to take a walk with him along a street bordering the foot hills. For privacy. A bright moon shed its hard light on snowpeaks, from up a ravine they could hear the weird yipyap of coyote howl, in the other direction a train whistle intermittently drifted up from the plains.

"There is a third force, we don't know what it is," Childers. "Of course I'm retired so I'm not completely au courant, you understand, there are things I don't know. Plenty. Things that nobody knows. My experience is that nobody knows the whole picture, they do it that way on purpose but somebody at the top is supposed to know, right. Only I don't think anybody does."

"The Colonel?"

"I doubt it, but maybe he thinks he does."

A clattering sound. Six or seven deer dashed across the street ahead of them.

"You have a right to know, but do you want to? Knowing just puts you at risk, the more you know the more the risk. Either they ignore you and isolate you so nobody takes you seriously or if they start taking you seriously maybe something will happen to you. I'm not necessarily talking about violence, lots of things can happen to you besides violence. Your income tax problems suddenly increase so you don't have time to think about anything else, or you can't get a job, or you get a wasting disease, or your wife finds out about your girlfriend, or your boss finds out about your sexual habits, or your house catches fire, or your pets suddenly die, or you get involved in a law suit, or your company transfers you to Milwaukee. And you'll never know what hit you, you'll just think, well, bad luck. You never consider that nothing is coincidence in the short run, though everything is coincidental in the long run."

"You're getting ahead of me," the investigator.

"I'm not ahead of you, the big bang was ahead of all of us, the original coincidence. Get with it. Everything is still happening at once, but at different places. Time is just extension through space. That's why anything you don't know is your own fault."

They heard a gun bang somewhere in the hills.

"What was that?"

"That?" Childers. "That was a shot in the dark. You hear them often in the hills. Poachers, maybe."

"Look, what is this all about?" the investigator.

"You really don't know? Then you don't want to know. It's about varmints, varmints and varmint control. You know what they do with varmints in the West, they shoot them."

"They've been shooting them for years, how many could be left?"

"In the West not many," Childers. "But in the cities. And the rest of the world, in Asia, Africa, Latin America, in Brazil, for example."

The investigator was beginning to get the idea. "They just shoot them?"

"Not exactly. Let's say they harvest them."

The investigator thought he was going to throw up but he didn't get the chance because Childers grunted, staggered as if he'd been hit with something heavy, then collapsed like dead meat. He was on the ground face up, mouth hanging open, left arm awkwardly under his body, a spreading red spot on his shirt where his tweed jacket had fallen open. There was a surprised look to his open eyes. The investigator dived into a shallow ditch along the road, the other side of the road was open to the foot hills. He froze for a minute then scrambled on all fours down the ditch. When he found a road cutting into the one he was on he got up and started running toward the town. Then he slowed to a fast walk and wandered around for a while looking for Childers' house where he'd left his rented car. His plan was to get to the airport as soon as possible, debating whether to even go back to the Boulderado to pick up his things. But when he found Childers' place there were flashing red lights and three fire trucks outside.

"We got a call for a fire here," a fireman said.

The investigator told them about it, they radioed for the police and he went on one of the trucks to help find where it had happened. But he couldn't. He was sure he'd found the right place but Childers wasn't there. A policeman questioned him, looked at him funny, and told him not to leave town for the time being. They told him keep it quiet don't talk to anyone about it.

When he got back to the Boulderado there was a woman waiting for him who he'd never seen before. She introduced herself as Stella Vortis, a well built forty year old in an expensive looking dress with an expensive looking shawl and blinkless eyes. Brown. What she wanted was to talk to him about Poe, she'd heard about the lecture, she hoped she wasn't barging in.

"Well okay," the investigator, "but not just now. Let's make an appointment."

"You don't understand," Stella, "I probably didn't explain it well enough. There's apparently a secret code in the writings of Poe that predicts what's going to happen to me day by day, and right now there's another crisis."

"Wait a minute."

"It's true. I know it's hard to believe but for example Poe predicted my liver disease a month before I found out about it. And that's where I first found out about the transplant. I had a liver transplant."

"I'm sorry but I . . ."

"That's alright, I'm fine now."

"Good but . . ."

"I can't drink alcohol. And I still have to take some drugs, but that's a small price to pay. Don't you think?"

"I, absolutely . . ."

"They replaced a kidney at the same time. Just one. The other one's alright. All this was very expensive, insurance didn't cover it. Luckily I have money. I say luckily because otherwise I might have waited for years and then it would have been too late. But I paid to get to the head of the Q, as the English say. And that's the problem."

"What?"

"That I'm running out of money. Something fishy is going on."

"What's that?"

"That's why I want you to help me with Poe. My accountants say my investments are turning sour, one of them said turning sour, but it's not their business to tell me what to do. But I can tell they think my broker is crooked and I need to do something else with the money. Only there's no way I can know for sure. Except through Poe."

"This is absurd," they were already on the stairs. "I'm exhausted I'm going to my room."

"It may be absurd but I'm going with you," she made a little motion with her arm but big enough to reveal a small gun in her hand under the shawl.

Once in the room she made him take his clothes off. "All of them," she stressed, "it makes me feel safer." Then, still holding the gun on him while he stood there she got down and started sucking his cock, though she interrupted herself shortly, "I know you're surprised but be good or I'll blow your balls off."

Under the circumstances he had a hard time getting an erection and besides his prostate hurt but after a while he began to get into it. She was good, very good. When he came he almost screamed, he just managed to hold it to a loud groan, dimly aware at the last second she slipped a plastic vial over his dick.

"Okay," she said, corking the vial and wiping it off. "That's that." She got up. "All the stuff about Poe was bullshit. Actually I'm from a satanic cult. Except I did have the transplants. In fact I also had a lung transplant, breast implants and a face lift while I was at it. What do you think of that?"

"You mind if I put on some clothes?" the investigator.

"Yes. I want you naked, I told you it makes me feel safer.

You know I'm not in the habit of doing this."

"Doing which?"

"Barging in on people," Stella.

"Then I guess I'm just lucky."

"You are lucky, I could have killed you. Did you think of that? I could still kill you, so keep a civil tongue in your face."

"What do you mean satanic cult?" the investigator.

"That's how I know Lena," she pulled a cross from under her blouse.

"And Lenna?"

"There is no Lenna. That's one of Lena's alternate personalities. Another is Lorna. And who knows who else. Lana I think. And Lola. She was abused you know, as a child. So was I. Pedophiles. It's routine for satanic cults, the sex hex, they destroy your i.d. it splits you schiz. Trained as a juvenile sex slave. There are a lot of us, it's as American as hot dogs. Remember that Denver society millionaire who'd been fucking his Miss America daughter since the age of five? Once you hit that highway you're on the interstate, no one ever knows what state they'll find you in. One minute I'm Stella, next minute who knows."

"What do you want?" the investigator.

"Want? I don't want anything. They want."

"They? Who? What?"

"Well I guess we'll just have to wait and see, won't we?" Stella.

"How will we know?"

"Well I suppose a little old carrier pigeon is just going to fly in with a message," Stella. "You can sit down now."

"You have to do what they say?"

"They still own the body parts, I just lease them. But they gave me a good package deal."

The investigator knew he was sort of in shock, but everything that was happening was beginning to seem completely normal to him, he was beginning to think he was in touch with some other rhythm of event than the one everyone else usually tuned in to. It was getting hard to keep track of what was happening in the world and what was happening in his head.

When the instructions finally came he was mildly suprised at the manner of delivery. Stella took a laptop out of her large handbag attached one cord to the television set another to the phone line.

"Let's turn on the TV while we're waiting," Stella. She pulled the drapes turned off lights picked up the zapper and did some channel surfing, ending up with CNN. Some story about thousands of people dying somewhere of something, or being killed, whatever it was there were bodies piled high like cordwood, being pushed into ditches by bulldozers.

Then the modem apparently kicked in and print appeared white on black: THIS IS THE MORTGAGE COMPANY COMMAND CENTER. OUR PROGRAMMING RUNS CONTINUOUSLY DESPITE OTHER SIMULTANEOUS APPLICATIONS. ITS OVER RIDE VIRUS CONVERTS YOUR ON-OFF TOGGLE INTO A FUNCTION KEY. PRESSING ONCE TWICE

THREE TIMES CORRESPONDS TO PRESSING ONE TWO OR THREE. FOR EXAMPLE IF YOU FEEL YOUR LIFE IS THREATENED PRESS ONE. IF YOU FEEL THE LIFE OF SOMEONE YOU LOVE IS THREATENED PRESS TWO. IF BOTH PRESS THREE. NOW WAIT FOR SUBSEQUENT COMMANDS. THE MORTGAGE COMPANY.

"We're waiting," Stella.

"Who's sending this?"

"All I know is they got a mortgage on my DNA."

The screen began to stir and brighten. THE MORTGAGE COMPANY IS AN OFFSHORE CONGLOMERATE WITH MULTINATIONAL OFFICES DEVOTED TO RAISING THE QUALITY OF YOUR LIFE. TO DO THIS WE ARE ATTEMPTING TO DEVELOP PATENTS ON CERTAIN SEQUENCES OF DNA. THIS MAY INCLUDE YOUR DNA AND THE DNA OF YOUR FRIENDS AND FAMILY. IF YOU FEEL COMFORTABLE WITH THIS PRESS ONE NOW. IF YOU FEEL UNCOMFORTABLE WITH THIS PRESS TWO NOW. THIS INFORMATION WILL BE ENTERED IN OUR DATA BASE. CURRENTLY WE ARE DEVELOPING VAST CRYOGENIC ORGAN AND SPERM BANKS FOR THE IMPROVEMENT OF THE RACE. IF YOU WOULD LIKE TO BECOME A DEPOSITOR IN OUR SPERM BANKS PRESS ONE NOW. YOU WILL BE SUPPLIED WITH A CHARMING HOSTESS AND AN APPROPRIATE RECEPTACLE. YOU WILL HAVE A GOOD TIME. IF YOU DO NOT LIKE GOOD TIMES PRESS TWO NOW. THIS INFORMATION WILL BE ENTERED IN OUR DATA BASE. IF YOU ARE A POTENTIAL ORGAN DONOR AND WOULD LIKE INFORMATION ON HOW TO PARTICIPATE IN OUR DONOR PRO-

GRAM PRESS ONE NOW. THIS MESSAGE WILL BE RE-PEATED UNTIL ALL PROGRAMMED CHOICES ARE PROP-ERLY INDICATED. WHERE CHOICES ARE NOT PROPERLY INDICATED LACK OF COOPERATION WILL BE ENTERED IN OUR DATA BASE. TO CONFIRM YOUR CHOICES PLEASE PRESS THE POUND SIGN PLEASE PRESS THE POUND SIGN PLEASE POUND THE PRESS SIGN PLEASE SIGN THE POUND PRESS PLEASE PRESS THE DOG POUND PLEASE SIGN DOG PLEASE

Then suddenly the screen started flashing ABORT ABORT ABORT went blank and the words INVISIBLE INC. appeared black on white.

"Wait a minute," Stella, "that's the wrong message."

As they watched the third "I" in INVISIBLE grew till it filled the screen, then turned into an eye.

"Something's wrong here," Stella, "I'm going to get in trouble."

"The third force is with you," said the speaker. "Check out WWW.ALTX.COM/OUT/OUT.HTML. Write it down, it helps. I heard it from the chain gang." He wrote it down. The screen went blank. Stella seemed distraught, the inves-tigator almost by reflex leaped off the bed the short dis-tance to the TV and grabbed her gun arm, the gun dropped, went off, they wrestled he naked, for some reason the det-onation gave him an erection pressed against her ass which she felt and raised her hands.

"Don't turn around," the investigator, "just walk over to the bed and lie face down."

"Don't shoot."

"My turn," he said, he pushed her skirt up underwear down her cunt was wet he plunged in she groaned, "Don't shoot," she repeated but he came almost instantaneously this time screaming but a forlorn scream she cursing him out.

After he kicked her out he called Vaca who said he'd meet him at a place on the mall, he found him there a while later at the bar chatting up a young blank faced thing, buxom, blond, "Don't you think you're a little old trying to service co-eds you pick up in bars?" the blond.

"Well, we start slower but we last longer," Vaca. He got up to join the investigator at a table, "Stay away from those fraternity gang bangs," he told her.

"Grade A meat head," to the investigator, "prime value on the hoof."

"You becoming a sexist in your old age?" the investigator.

"I'm sexist she's ageist," Vaca. "What about you?"

"Me? I don't have any vices."

"Right," Vaca. "I asked Dee Quonset to meet us here."

"Whose side is he on?"

"What sides?" Vaca. "Way I see it, Childers is on the wrong side because he's dead and I definitely want to be on the right side anymore."

"Yeah, well I'm on your side there," the investigator. "What happened to him?"

"Those mysterious helicopters. If you'd a stuck around you might've found out."

"Or I might have found myself on the wrong side," the investigator. "What do I do now? The police don't want me to leave town."

"You should a gat when the gatting was good."

"Now you tell me," the investigator.

"This is your life, amigo."

Quonset sat down. "Ciao muchacho," Vaca. What you been up to, Dee?"

"Little this, little that."

"Little target practice maybe?" Vaca.

"Wait a minute," Quonset.

"Well, you said you were a good shot," Vaca. "Hey, I been meaning to ask you, you related to the man invented the Quonset Hut?"

"An uncle. Man named Hut as it happens. You don't really think I dusted Childers."

"Just asking," Vaca. "So Childers' brother is in town. What, for the funeral?"

"What funeral, there's no body," Quonset.

"I guess that's why he's in town. I hear Trench is in Brazil," Vaca.

"And they're rounding up a refrigerator truck," Quonset.

"The Colonel?"

"Yeah. That means a meat shipment is due," Quonset.

"Probably," Vaca.

The investigator didn't want to ask what kind of meat shipment because he thought he knew.

"I think it's time to mount an operation," Vaca.

Quonset, "Okay . . . What?"

"I'm thinking . . ." Someone came up to the table, he looked just like Childers but maybe a little different, "You Vaca?"

"Jesus, you could be Childers' ghost," the investigator. Vaca, "This here's Quonset. And the investigator."

"I've met Dee."

"So he told you we'd be here," the investigator.

"No, just coincidence. I happened to be wandering around, been in a couple of bars. I recognized Dee."

"Amazing," Vaca.

"You're here because of your brother's . . ." The investigator.

"Yes, my brother's. That's the question. I also thought I might get in a little skiing, they tell me there's snow in the mountains."

"That's right," Vaca. "Excuse me for saying so, but you don't seem real broke up over your brother."

"We never got along. To tell you the truth I didn't like him much and haven't seen him in years. But there are probate problems, family problems, for one I'm looking for a will."

Childers' brother was a little shorter than Childers maybe, and maybe a little fatter. Maybe his hair was greyer. Or maybe not. Certainly he looked older.

"Well," Quonset, "you probably won't find it in the Boulder bars but I guess they're a fun place to look."

"No, I was looking for my daughter, she goes to school here. I was supposed to meet her in one of these places but

I forget which . . . wait a minute. There she is," standing up, "Lois!"

A blond at the bar, there were several, turned around, smiled, stood up and came over, "Dad, where've you been?"

"I lost the address. Let me introduce you to . . ."

"Hi," Vaca. She sort of looked like the young girl he'd been talking to though her face seemed a little different, "Hi," she smiled sweetly.

The others introduced themselves, Vaca trying to figure out whether it was the same girl or not. The bar was getting crowded. A wide variety of specimens, businessmen, hippies, fratrats with buccaneer bandannas, body art punks drifted back and forth or suddenly darted from one place to another, every once in a while a fortuitous knot would gather in one place among the hanging ferns and potted plants, the investigator wondered whether it amounted to a kind of human Brownian motion. As in a tank of tropical fish certain momentary coincidences of the colorful scatter jumped out at you as if they might have been composed. A couple in his line of sight moved revealing the tall thin Asian of the men's room, an instant later he was eclipsed and when the gap reopened he was gone and Vaca was introducing him to a woman something about whom sent ice down his spine, "Madame Lazonga." Her eyes were electric and her voice, when she greeted him, seemed to come from inside his head.

"Madame Lazonga is a psychic. I thought she'd come in handy for the Childers situation. She helped find my wife."

"What wife was that? Lorna?"

"So I was doing a number," Vaca. "A sting. It brought them out of the wood work, some of them."

"You should have told me."

"Don't you play poker? Where'd she go? You know she looks a lot like you?"

"Maybe she's in the ladies' room. You know her well?" the investigator.

"Very. We had an abortion together once. She has this way of disappearing and appearing all of a sudden."

Snowt appeared, "He wants to see you, Mr. Vaca."

"Who wants to see me?"

"Mr. Golden. I gather your wife is out of danger."

"What wife? I believe I used to have a wife but I don't think I have one now. But thanks for your help, it's good to know who's connected around here."

"As soon as possible. Tonight."

"Tell him to relax," Vaca. "Tell him I'm in no hurry."

"Mr. Golden isn't going to like that."

"Then tell him to go fuck himself." Snowt walked out.

Stay away from that one, the investigator heard Lazonga's voice but where was Lazonga? looking around. "Did you just see Lazonga?" to Vaca.

"No, she left," so the voice was in his head? He's dangerous because he isn't really there, it said. Nobody home. What's the danger? the investigator in his head. This dialogue was scary, but he didn't try to stop it either. He thought maybe she'd performed something like instant hypnosis on him.

People like that can do anything, the voice continued. They can kill you without thinking about it. Maybe it's not so bad if that's what you want.

Why would you think that?

I'm sort of cozying up to death myself, as an ally.

One part of his head talking to another part? The investigator, worried that he was getting schizzy, walked out of the bar, dark now, sidewalks deserted, bats swooped in and out of streetlight illumination, suddenly a big one heading straight toward him, shark mouth, drool foaming, the investigator ducked and cringed, the thing was gigantic as it whooshed over his shoulder banked circled and came back, it seemed to be growing, he could see disgusting individual hairs whiskering its blind face, it was heading for his eyes as he covered them he felt something soft and slimy brush his ear, then nothing. Something shaking him, Vaca's voice, he opened his eyes. Vaca had him by the shoulder.

"You having the DTs or something? What's happening?"

"Nothing, I just had this horrible hallucination."

"Like what?"

"A giant bat attacking me."

"Oh, the bat," Vaca. "I saw the bat too."

"You . . .?"

"Sure. The famous Boulder bat? It only attacks tourists, but usually on Halloween. What was it doing out tonight?"

"What is it?" the investigator.

"Nobody knows for sure, some people think it's a messenger of death, others that it's a civic guardian against over-development, still others that it's the spirit of Chief Left Hand. They say it sucks the blood of tourists and real estate developers and turns them into wandering green-peaceniks who can never die. Or maybe it's just a fig meant for your imagination."

"I see, you're putting me on," the investigator.

"Don't worry about it, amigo, people have always seen weird things out West. Mirages. It's mostly desert and the desert's a blank slate."

"I am worried about it," the investigator.

"Forget all this stuff. What you don't understand can drive you crazy. Let's go see Golden."

"I thought you let him know you weren't coming to-night."

"Sure, that's why I want to go tonight. Keep them off balance."

They took Vaca's truck. When they arrived they found Snowt and Crow with Golden.

"If you fellas were having a pow-wow," Vaca, "we can go back down the mountain."

"Now that you're here," Golden. "What can I get you?" he rang for someone.

"Wouldn't mind a single malt," Vaca. "That's what the investigator here always drinks, and he comes from the big city. Guess you're all rattled about Childers, wasn't he a friend of yours?"

"I have a lot of friends," Golden. "Childers, Trench, one is as good as another. I want to offer you a business deal, what with the Feds threatening to steal our grazing land. I'm a straight shooter. A million and a half for your spread."

"Shee, I couldn't take that. That land ain't worth but half."

"All right, I'll give you half."

"That's more like it, but what would happen to my cows, they gotta have a place too."

"I want the cows," Golden. "Throw in the cows, I'll double the price."

"I'm kinda fond of my cows."

"All right, what do you want?"

"I don't want nothin. What do you want?" Vaca.

"See," Crow, "we're kind of nervous about depending on your cooperation, given that you're not by nature very cooperative."

"Oh, no. You got me all wrong. I mean if you think I'm being uncooperative I'm really sorry I want to cooperate, I really do, only sometimes I get little confused about what we're cooperating on, so maybe you can let me in on it."

"You're already in on it and you can't get out," Crow.

"That's probably true," Vaca.

"Shut up Crow," Golden. "The Golden Eagles are coming back, you have them on your spread."

"I've noticed, near that little lake. Every year."

"What I want to do with your property is start a Golden Eagle preserve. That's all. I want to call it the Golden Eagle Ranch, I've talked it over with my press agent. Put in a few head of buffalo, some llamas for the kids to ride, a farm animal petting zoo, stock a trout pond, get the tourists com-

ing through. Throw in a little panning for gold we can probably run the whole thing at a profit and it's ecological too."

"Make up for the eagles your boys've been shooting on
your ranch land," Vaca.

"Well, we need to protect the live stock. We're popping
them from air planes now, I even tried it from a glider once.
Boy, there's a fun sport, with a glider you can get right up
close, fly along with them and then, poom! they drop like
stones."

"Yeah."

"That's right. So if you ever change your mind you'll
know you're helping to save the Golden Eagle, be a patriotic act," Golden. "Meantime I guess we'll just keep on
trucking like we've been trucking."

Lenna or Lena drifted in from some other part of the
house, sensational in a string bikini, Golden got up and put
an arm around her. "Time for us to go and play around the
pool, hope we'll be seeing you boys soon." She gave the investigator a long, hot look as she went out in front of
Golden steering her with a hand on the back of her neck,
every man jackoff watching her bare round ass follow her
out the door.

On the way down, Vaca, "He wants the cows. Interesting."

"Why so?"

"He's got plenty cows. But he wants these cows. Yeah."

"So?"

"Whata these cows got that other cows don't got?"

"What?" the investigator.

"Radiation. According to Leonard."

"Too bad he didn't get a chance to finish that study."

"Maybe that's why he didn't get a chance," Vaca. "Sheez, an I been thinking all along what they wanted was an air strip."

"There's a word we use in literary criticism, 'overdetermined.' Meaning when there's more than one reason for a given result."

"Overdetermined, yeah. Makes something sort of inevitable don't it? I always knew you'd come through as an investigator. But who's he working for?"

"Golden? I thought you thought he was working for the Feds?"

"I'm beginning to wonder maybe they're working for him. I been thinking, what's the most valuable mineral resource now in these here mountains?"

"Gold? Oil?"

"Refined weapons grade plutonium," Vaca.

"So?"

"Just something to think about."

Back at the Boulderado there was a message for the investigator. The clerk read it off a piece of paper, "It's from Mork," giving the investigator an amused look. "Of 'Mork and Mindy'?"

"Who are they?" the investigator.

"They were a TV series done in Boulder. Sci fi."

"Why here?"

"Because it's like a different planet? It just says, 'You're next.' That mean anything to you?"

"Right," the investigator. "It means I'm about to be kidnapped by flying saucers."

Up in his room he checked out WWW.ALTX.COM/OUT/ OUT.HTML. He found himself online in a text called OUT, hoping it showed a way out, but was interrupted by a call from Dee Quonset, "Childers's brother?"

"Yes?"

"His daughter. Been kidnapped by flying saucers."

"You don't expect me to take this seriously?" the investigator.

"That's what the kidnap note said. There have been sightings around here."

"Signed by Mork?"

"Hey, how did you know?" Dee.

"Who is it?"

"We're trying to find out. We did a search on Snowt and Crow. They were both born in Roswell, New Mexico on July 4, 1947."

"Isn't that where that UFO crashed?" the investigator.

"And when," Dee.

"With the ET's still in it?"

"You got it," Dee.

The investigator hung up and turned away from the phone, there was a thing hanging in mid air, bright green covered with mucousy tentacles and feelers, glob shaped, fanged indefinite mouth, a couple of red eyes that kept changing places and it scared the shit out of him. Not because he was afraid of it but because he knew he was imagining it. It sort of evaporated and he turned on the TV, local news, half listening when there was a flash that some plutonium was unaccounted for at Rocky Flats nobody was sure how much. His prostate was bothering him, it was his body's way of registering psychosomatic tension, next it would be eye strain then worst of all TMJ if he didn't do something to relieve it.

The TV screen went to ads then flashed: INVISIBLE INC. As he watched the third "I" in INVISIBLE grew till it filled the screen, then turned into an eye. The phone rang he picked up the receiver. One of those synthesized voices he couldn't even tell whether it was male or female: "We're watching you. We care about you. You need to mount an operation. Watch for your chance. We'll be there to help. Remember, you aren't alone. There are a lot of us. We're everywhere. And nowhere. On the net. And check your e-mail."

The investigator wasn't sure what was happening or what he was imagining. Things like this never happened to him in New York. Maybe it was the mile high thin air that had the same effect as alcohol reducing oxygen supply to the brain. He felt as if he were being engulfed by the New Age with all its smart, shoddy superstitions which he'd always considered signs of collective mental breakdown. He hated himself every time he consulted the I-Ching, even in the past when it was hip. That he was now slipping over the edge he knew and if the voices in his head continued he'd have to figure he'd lost it.

The TV screen was back to local news. There was a brief report that the unaccounted for plutonium at Rocky Flats was now accounted for because in fact it had not been unaccounted for.

We need to think about Childers' brother's daughter, said Madame Lazonga in his head. My crystal ball shows they didn't kidnap her they recruited her. Like Patty Hearst, sex was the lolly pop. But it looks like their first mistake, Lazonga. Right, if they mistook Childers' brother for Childers, he said to Madame Lazonga in his head.

That's right, said the voice in his head, so what we need to do now is meet with them to arrange an exchange.

But an exchange for what? he asked in his head.

Exactly, said the voice in his head, we need a lolly pop.

He checked his e-mail on his laptop. There was a message that said, "Call this number for shiatsu prostate massage— InInc." Followed by a phone number. How did they know about his prostate? He wondered if the room was bugged then remembered he hadn't said anything aloud about his health. Unless he'd been talking to himself. Or maybe his head was bugged.

He called the number for the shiatsu prostate massage. Why not?

"Third Eye Body Works," a woman's voice, bell clear.

"Is this the number for a garage or a massage?" the investigator.

A little laugh, "We work on your corporeal body, for your auto body you have to get someone else." He decided he liked this person.

"Well I have prostate trouble, eye strain and a dent in my left fender." He felt better already.

"You come right over we'll see what we can do."

He came right over, and when he arrived she saw what she could do. Anything she wanted because as far as the investigator was concerned it was love at first sight. His feelings went totally labile. An aura kept appearing and disappearing around her blond head and the oddest thing was when he looked at her sidelong she appeared to have pointed animal ears. Also her eyes, which were green, seemed to focus not on his physical self but on his psychic self, he couldn't explain it, but this already seemed like one of the strangest and most interesting things that had ever happened to him. She was very tall but her body, in a floating green gown, seemed almost not to be there, she was all head and her head all eyes. What happened next was scary, he thought he was seeing it but knew he couldn't be, there was a puff of smoke under her feet and her figure began to rise slowly like a space shuttle starting to blast off as she smiled benignly down at him. She then settled back to earth and led him to a massage table, "Time to get to work," she said and it was only then that he realized he'd almost forgotten about his aches and pains. He clicked on the option he was dealing with a saucerian but rammed head-on into common sense.

She gave him a towel, asked him to undress and lie on the table, left the room. The inspector undressed but undressing gave him an erection. He lay down with the towel over his embarrassingly stubborn organ.

"My name is Libby," coming back in, "don't you think that's a pretty name? What we're doing here, we're mounting an operation. You need to be part of the operation. Because I'm the fairy godmother of abused children. What you do I'm going to tell you soon. As soon as you relax. As soon as you relax. As soon as you fall asleep. Look into my eyes, that's right, as soon as you fall asleep. Asleep. My eyes. Asleep. Asleep."

But the investigator never fell asleep, at least as far as he knew, the next thing he knew in fact he was wide awake, relaxed, his prostate had never felt better, his eyes were super sharp only his erection had mysteriously disappeared he wondered how.

Libby was standing over him smiling, "You feel good now don't you?"

"I feel very good, when do I get the treatment?"

"But you don't need the treatment if you don't need the treatment you don't get the treatment."

The investigator was a little disappointed even though he felt very good. "Can I come back some other time and get the treatment?"

"You surely can," Libby. "You surely will."

"And you said there was the possibility of some sort of operation?"

"For that information you need to speak to the operator."

"What operator?"

"At our main office, Invisible Inc. They'll contact you."

"You said you were going to tell me what to do."

"You already know what to do," Libby.

"What do I owe you?"

"You owe nothing to me. You owe it to yourself."

The investigator left a little mystified trying to figure out what he knew he was supposed to do and how he would know when to do it. But he didn't have time for too much introspection he used to introspect a lot but now events were moving too fast and there were too many of them. He kept thinking about Childers' brother's daughter, but didn't know why or what to do about her.

He got back to the Boulderado later than he thought it was already night. There was a man in his room, the man was watching television. When the investigator walked in the man looked up in surprise. The investigator was just as surprised. "What . . ." they both said at the same time then at the same time broke off. The man looked very familiar but the investigator couldn't place him at first. Suddenly the investigator realized that the man looked just like him. His next thought was a mind stopper maybe the man was him. And if he was him who was he?

Panic. The investigator seemed to be caught in a vacuum and lost consciousness. When he regained consciousness someone was knocking at the door and the other man was gone. Or was it he who was gone, he had no way of knowing. He recalled being told the Microbiology Department at the University specialized in cloning. Absurd thought. Except that woman who'd raped him in his hotel room had stolen some of his DNA.

He opened the door and let in How Ling. How Ling congratulated him. When the investigator asked about what, he told him that Childers' brother's daughter had been rescued and that the investigator had rescued her. The investigator couldn't believe it. What was the lolly pop? the investigator wanted to know, violence was the lolly pop How Ling informed him. Without even asking Childers' brother the investigator had pretended he was Childers' brother, he had imitated his voice on the phone and arranged a meeting. The kidnappers were not so stupid as to arrange a personal meeting they sent a representative, a Brazilian who couldn't speak any English. The investigator couldn't speak any Portuguese so all they could do was exchange certain notes each by arrangement had prepared in advance the Brazilian's by a translator. The investigator's first note said, 'What do you want?'

The Brazilian handed him a note in exchange that said, 'I don't know where she is don't ask me.'

The meeting took place at night on a farm out on the plains, according to How Ling, at the edge of what seemed to be a field of grain, probably corn by the smell, it rustled like an ocean with every breath of wind. You had to take a narrow dirt road to get there. The senses registered vast extensions of space in every direction. It was very dark and it was hard to read the notes. They weren't allowed any lights for security reasons so the investigator, reading by moonlight, wasn't always sure he was reading the notes correctly, particularly since the Brazilian's seemed to be written in childish block letters probably with someone's left hand to disguise the writing.

The investigator asked How Ling how he knew all this and How Ling told the investigator he was following him as usual and had no idea what was about to happen till it happened.

The investigator's second note, according to How Ling, said, 'First I have to be sure she's alive and well.'

In exchange the Brazilian's note said, 'Never has been so hidden your daughter so what.'

The investigator's next note said, 'I will go with you if you want.'

The Brazilian's, 'Next to your daughter is healthy including sex.'

The investigator's, 'I will tell you what you want if you tell me what it is.'

The Brazilian's, 'She is a very good one. She likes it.'

The investigator, 'If I were you I would let her go and not try anything funny, we know who you are.'

The Brazilian, 'She have a lot of fun with us, no hurry.'

The investigator, 'If it's money I can get it.'

The Brazilian, 'Call off everything, she died. Or else.'

The investigator, 'Every move you make is being followed.'

The Brazilian, 'At first cry, now have new leash. We can wait. It is already tomorrow.'

But the investigator was losing patience, he was out of notes. He had a jack handle from the car on the ground next to him, picked it up and swung for the Brazilian's head, crunch, the man went down like lead with barely a sound.

"You are surprised it so easy," How Ling concluded, "but sometimes is, sometimes it extremely hard. Killing a man."

Pause.

"I walky-talky Invisible Inc.," How continued. "Others come, find clue on body, we go to place free daughter."

"I killed somebody?"

"You kill, or some other you," How.

There was a knock on the door, it was Childers' brother's daughter. "I go now," How.

"I just came to thank you," Childers' brother's.

"No problem." She looked different. The poor kid looked beat. Worn. As the investigator recalled, she used to look the image of many bland blond co-eds though he'd only met her once.

"It wasn't easy for me. They were trying to recruit me, though they said I was a little old. You got there just in time."

"Lucky. How old are you?"

"Going on seventeen. They raped me you know. A lot. Like Patty Hearst they said. I was almost starting to like it, that's why you were just in time."

"Damned lucky."

"They all wore cartoon character masks. Mickey Mouse kept telling me not to worry because he was my dad. But I know he wasn't. He was just imitating his voice, don't you think so?"

"Of course."

"Do you think it would have been terrible if I had started to like it?"

"Yes and no," the investigator.

"I felt so disloyal. It was like there were two of me."

"I wouldn't worry about it," the investigator.

"They said it was my fault, do you think it was my fault? I feel so guilty."

"You shouldn't feel guilty, it wasn't your fault. It was their fault. They should feel guilty."

"But they don't. Whose fault is that?"

"I don't know, I feel guilty," the investigator. "Maybe it's my fault. Maybe it's zeitgeist's fault."

"Do you think, since you rescued me from liking it, that you should make me like it yourself?"

"No, I don't think so, I think you should go home now."

"All right. Thank you."

"You already thanked me," the investigator.

"No I mean for not raping me. I would have let you do it."

"I know. But you should avoid bad habits. And you're welcome."

She left. Sick kid, he thought, but she'd had a tough break. The voice in his head said, Stay away from schizzy people, you can't trust them, you can't pin them down, you never know when they're going to come back at you because you never know who they are. Madame Lazonga again.

I never know who I am, he answered in his head, from one minute to the next. Does that mean I should stay away from myself?

Vaca called, asked to meet him in a nearby bar. "Why always in bars?" the investigator.

"Bars are hard to bug. Besides, I like to drink."

Dee was also there when he got there. "We got an idea of the personnel for the incoming," Quonset. "Trench, the two Spics and a local name of Jimmy Hunch, you know him?"

Vaca whistled. "Hunch, he's a bad injun. Half breed I think. Got a chip on his shoulder, probably a buffalo chip."

"Against who?"

"Against the world. I don't like to tangle with him."

"Who says we have to?" the investigator. "Takes two to tangle."

"You know what they're doing down there?" Quonset.

"Who? Where?" the investigator.

"These guys?" Quonset. "In Brazil? And not only Brazil?"

"What?"

"The locals shoot homeless children in the street down there. Like rats. They're considered pests, varmints, they happen to be human but that's the only difference."

"Yeah," the investigator, "I read something about it in the papers."

"Right. They hire off duty cops and stuff who run an extermination service. Only it's getting too hot an item for the local politicos so now they hire foreigners, hunting parties that fly in and get out fast. Using drug routes. They even, christ, have started selling high price safari tickets to millionaires who want that ultimate thrill of hunting the human animal. There's a lot of money in it."

"And the biggest bucks are in the organ trade," Vaca.

"You mean . . ."

"Sure. Why waste them? They always take this doctor along, well actually he's a licensed veterinarian, but he's very good with the knife. A Doctor Greul, he's a small animal specialist."

The investigator, "How do I know this is true?"

"You don't."

"Or that somebody as big as Golden would get involved in something like that."

"I'll tell you," Quonset, "you know how in Eastern Europe since the commies crashed the most successful capitalists are the big time criminals?"

"So?"

"What makes you think it's different here? Besides, Golden's got other motives. For him they butcher them a little differently. There's a locker up at his place they say can preserve meat indefinitely. It seems he has strange tastes."

The investigator felt sick. In a number of ways for a number of reasons. "Why are you telling me all this?"

"Because it's too late for you now," Quonset. "You've lost your last protection which was your innocence. So you're part of it. Because you know too much. The only thing you can do is cooperate and keep your fingers crossed."

The investigator knew it was true but it sounded like a suicide trip. He was out of his territory and without landmarks, needed a reference point, thought, on the way out of the bar, maybe Lavigne, at least partly from familiar ground, might be the person to talk to.

Whatever else you might say about Lavigne he was smart, the investigator thought, maybe too smart. And always aware of the lay of the land, the way the wind was blowing, the weather of the culture. He was one of the first academics to pick up on computers and did an early computer study of Swift that proved he was a satirist. Now he was involved with artificial intelligence but not in machines in people. He was researching the question of whether people could be instilled with artificial intelligence thereby making them more manipulable. He was discovering that many college educated people already functioned on the basis of artificial intelligence because that's what they taught in the colleges and especially the professional schools. Maybe that was why the investigator had the feeling about Lavigne that there was something missing there, that there were a lot of things Lavigne left out because that was the mark of artificial intelligence, leaving things out, leaving anything out that wasn't immediately profitable.

He called Lavigne from the Boulderado but he didn't exactly know what to ask him because he didn't exactly know what he wanted to know, that was what Lavigne was supposed to tell him to begin with. So what he asked him was something that made no sense even to the investigator himself in fact he wasn't even sure why he asked, what he asked Lavigne was whether he thought it was better to put everything in or leave everything out.

Long pause.

The investigator, "I mean ideally of course, theoretically."

"Did you know Lazonga?" Lavigne.

"Did?"

"She's dead. Hit by a truck."

"She didn't see it coming?"

"Guess not," Lavigne.

"I thought she was supposed to be a psychic."

"She was. She was working with a journalist on a lead about missing plutonium at Rocky Flats."

The investigator was desolated, he didn't exactly know why, he hardly knew her at all, just glimpsed her once really. Maybe he was more disappointed than desolated, disappointed because he'd thought at least somebody had some privileged way of knowing stuff, somebody could still get a sense of the big picture maybe and figure out from what was happening today what might happen tomorrow, but that was all out the window now. The picture window.

"And in answer to your question," Lavigne, "I think it's better to put everything in, because inclusion is better than exclusion, the big picture. But you can't. So practically speaking you have to leave everything out except what's absolutely relevant. It's the only way to get anything done."

He sort of knew what Lavigne was talking about. But something else was troubling him. He was still feeling guilty about killing somebody. If he did kill somebody, because there was only one witness and it wasn't he himself, so he guessed he felt guilty in case he killed somebody. Life was getting so ambiguous it was getting him completely off balance and he was glad when the desk called and asked if they could send a Mr. Ling up so he didn't have to think about it any more.

How said Libby wanted to see him the investigator said he was in no mood he explained why. How said no problem he would give him a treatment lie down. He said he carried his needles with him.

"What needles."

"Acupuncture needles. So. Question is guilty or not guilty. The answer maybe not one but both." Ling had him take off his shirt and turn over, he felt what seemed like pin pricks on various areas of his body followed by a prickly sensation followed by drowsiness when he woke up and turned over How wasn't there he was there. Again. He himself. Or his other self, whoever he was, standing there in the middle of the room. He forced himself into a mode of extreme self consciousness by which he was just barely able to verify that he himself was still there and that the other was still other but he could tell that the distinction was slipping.

"So," he said. "You're feeling guilty. So what?"

"The question is not whether I'm feeling guilty but whether I am guilty," he answered. "We're talking murder."

"Murder is the initial act of civilization, it's all down hill from there."

"Let's not talk philosophy, I'm talking here and now. I've got a situation."

"I understand you got a situation. It's a youdunnit. Either you done it or I done it."

"Or somebody else done it."

"That's not my concern."

"What is?"

"If you dunnit I didn't."

"Right, if you dunnit I didn't."

"It's settled then."

The investigator was relieved that it was settled. Only he was unsettled because he no longer knew who the investigator was. One of them said goodbye and walked out but he no longer knew whether it was him or the other.

Maybe it doesn't matter, a voice in his head, who said that? then realized it was Lazonga's voice in his head. But Lazonga was dead so he was surprised she had an opinion about it. Maybe being dead didn't matter to her.

How came back in, "We have names."

"Whose names?"

"The safari. Abdurado Al Mohammed, Glenn Gebhard, Adolf Jose Muller Berdal, Hector Lugo Dupont, Cenon Mario Clarke, Ahmed Nagi Abubaker, Michel Jel Carlos. Besides Trench."

"Those are all aliases of Carlos the terrorist, I read them in the paper."

"Y-e-e-s. But now he caught others can use. We go now."

Over at Libby's office Libby wasn't there, the investigator was introduced to a young woman named Athena Chipmunk. She said she was a professional T'ai Chi instructor but was a member of Invisible Inc. She said that as a Native

American she had certain connections and she was going to introduce him to Hunch the halfbreed. She said that she was a halfbreed herself but many people didn't like that term. She said that Hunch on the other hand liked calling himself a halfbreed because he said almost all Americans are halfbreeds of one sort or another. She said he believed that's why the socalled White race is going to phase out of existence. She said he believed that the same thing is going to happen with religions and that everyone is going to end up Judeobuddhic, which is what he was. She said that Boulder is the world center of Judeobuddhism.

Jews becoming Buddhists are like nuns becoming nudists, Lazonga's voice in his head.

They drove in the investigator's rental car up through a canyon into a wind that had him struggling to keep the car on the road, especially when it turned to hard dirt washboard shaking their spines. The investigator panicked on a steep switchback when the car stalled in second, the emergency wouldn't hold when he tried to restart it, he finally got going by flooring it in first after a short scary rollback toward a cliff, the wind tearing at them all the time. When they drove up to Hunch's house the investigator was surprised because it wasn't a house. It was a postmodern mansion mushrooming on a cliff overlooking a ponderosa filled valley, gleaming white but looking like it had been organically grown. Athena Chipmunk explained that it was made of some special foam concrete that allowed for organic curvilinear shapes some local architect liked to experiment with.

"You expected he'd be living in some patchwork wickiup in front of a camp fire and a pinto tethered to a tree," Athena. "Or maybe even in an igloo."

They rang at the door and were buzzed in it was like walking into a cave or a throat with curved and sloping walls round windows at irregular intervals snaking intestinal chambers. Then around a curve to a light filled room with glass on one side overlooking the valley. On the opposite wall the view was reflected by several Victorian looking gold framed mirrors that seemed out of place.

Hunch walked in his arm sweeping toward the view, as if to say, How about that.

"You like my collection of mirrors?" Hunch. "I collect gilt mirrors."

The investigator made an approving sound.

Hunch was a big nosed, coffee colored Indian looking man, muscular, squat, with an aggressive chin. The investigator noticed he was left handed. He was wearing jeans, moccasins, leather vest with no shirt, a flashy turquoise necklace and a pig tail. He offered them the famous local national brand herb tea, said he gets it free from the man who makes it, "An acquaintance from the business community."

The investigator felt his eyebrows rising.

"Why not?" Hunch. "I'm a business man. I'm in pharmaceuticals. Drugs are pharmaceuticals."

"I didn't . . ."

"Never mind, you thought a guy like me got to be into something crooked because I'm half redskin. Worse, I'm also half nigger and half kike. So I got to be some kind of buccaneer, right? What I am is an entrepreneur, a free range marketeer. A capitalist cowboy."

"I thought . . ."

"Look, it's crazy. They even try to stop us using peyote in rituals. But we got a redskin senator now, all that gonna change maybe. Stop making pushy laws for somebody else's good, like motorcycle helmets, which he don't like because he rides too."

"Then why . . ."

"Why I want to see you because I need your help. See Golden and us we cooperate but now he's getting funny. We think maybe he's trying to go around us, we think he's into something bigger."

"Who killed . . . "

"Not us. We're not doing all the killing around here. We're just trying to do business, but there's something out-side going on. This is a different kind of thing, something high tech with some kind of, what you call, ideology in-volved. You know what I'm saying? Like, who's this Colo-nel? Crazy stuff. Cattle mutilations that kind of crap. What's cattle mutilations got to do with what we hear they're smuggling musical instruments and shit, shit, how much could you make? And it started just coincidentally around the time you rode into town."

"Now wait a minute I . . ."

"Never mind I know what you're going to say. So don't say it. I'm not asking you to tell me anything now. Think about it. Take your time. Twelve hours, maybe even twenty-four, we'll be in touch. And don't get nervous, we all got to die some day so why not tomorrow?"

"The truth is . . ."

"That's right. The truth is that the gringo been exploiting everybody for years, so this is a way of exploiting back. But maybe the gringo is caught in his own system of exploitation. That's Golden's problem. You think I'm a dummy because I'm a halfbreed? You surprised I talk this way? Shit! it's as plain as the nose on my face."

"I didn't think that because . . ." stopping in midsentence in walked Lenna or Lena or was it just Lena. Said hello and sidled up to Hunch in a way made it clear they were intimate, the knife of jealousy went right through the investigator's stomach and twisted a couple of times. It was unmistakable and he was surprised, he didn't know he was jealous of her but realized it had been true when he saw her with Golden too. From which he understood he was in love. It sort of shocked him, especially since he was already in love with Libby. Lenna or Lena. And he didn't even know who she was.

"I know you're surprised to see me here," Lenna or Lena, "but I can't help it. It's between Hunch and Todd."

"Golden?"

"You see it out there?" Hunch, his arm around Lenna or Lena ignoring her conversation. "So many beautiful things you can't take it all in. It starts here with the Front Range and goes all the way to the Pacific. Sometimes thisall's so beautiful you don't care if you die."

You want to die even, Lazonga in his head. Because thisall makes you enlarge your frame of reference. And death is the largest frame of reference.

"And you know what we're going to do with it? Casinos. Like the new ones up in Central City. Or on the reservations. It's the new gold rush. So when you want to tell us what Golden is into call. What is it, arms? Rocky Flats? the Feds? Whatever it is it's starting to make us ordinary crooks feel like small potatos. That's all, now I got to go. I'm half Buddhist, I got to do my prostrations."

"You do prostrations?" the investigator.

Hunch belly laughing, "It's good for my prostate," as he disappeared through a vaginal hallway with Lenna or Lena looking over her shoulder at the investigator a mock help-me expression elevating her brows. He heard Hunch laugh again he had a laugh like no tomorrow.

The investigator left with an uneasy feeling, he didn't feel like the most popular boy on the block. He felt like it was time to get out but he knew it was too late to get out because apart from everything else he no longer wanted to go back.

"Well, looks like I'm offered twelve to twenty-four hours all around," to Athena Chipmunk back in the car.

But Athena Chipmunk wasn't listening, she had a funny concentrating look on her face, maybe she was masturbat-ing her hands were folded over her crotch and her breathing was heavy. A stream of vapor came out of her mouth inflating like a balloon. In it words appeared: Nothing much is left but to cozy up to death. He knew right away what it was what it was was a conscious hallucination, something like a mirage, he'd had them before but not so often as recently. He knew it was Lazonga speaking to him but he reached over and shook Athena Chipmunk by her shoulder.

"What are you doing?" The investigator.

Athena, "Mental T'ai Chi. This is how I compose my poetry."

"Poetry."

"I workshop at the Jack Kerouac School of Disembodied Poetics. Study with Ginny."

"Kinney?"

"Allen. Ginsberg."

The wind shook the car he was negotiating down the hairpins in first thinking about Lenna or Lena. He sort of liked being in love and he sort of didn't. He sort of liked it because he liked being surprised and he sort of didn't because he knew it was a hopeless proposition.

"You want to meet him?" Athena.

"Who?"

"Ginny, I have an appointment."

"Oh. Sure."

He knew that being in love with Lenna or Lena was like a death trip because who was she? Being in love with someone who you didn't know who it was was like being on a trip to nowhere.

"He's a Judeobuddhist," Athena.

"Good. What's Judeobuddhism?"

"It combines the moral doctrine of Judaism with the cosmic wisdom of Buddhism." He looked at her she was kind of cute. Had the right instincts too he was getting to like Athena. A lot.

"Also, I'm studying The Tibetan Book of the Dead," Athena.

"Yes, well people are dying all over the world now. In gross lots. Mass market murder, it's the coming thing," the investigator. "And we're all linked to the mass market, locked to its chains."

You'll be sure to hold your breath at the putrid stench of death. Lazonga.

Down to Boulder an old school building now the Buddhist Naropa Institute the investigator went in with her Ginsberg was there busy talking to people she introduced him.

"What kind of religion is Judeobuddhism?" the investigator.

"Buddhism is not a religion it's a practice," Ginny, then kissed him on the mouth and smiled. It felt hairy the investigator didn't know what to make of it. The pronouncement or the kiss.

"What did he mean by that?" the investigator.

"He meant it's not supernatural it's cosmic. Cosmic is real," Athena.

The red head with the motorcycle jacket was there he pulled the investigator aside, "We want to thank you."

"For what? I didn't do anything," the investigator.

"The girl. You do what you can. See, to be a link in the chain you have to break it. Mutilation, emasculation, violation, vivisection, forced incest, cannibalism, obligatory rape, bodies hacked to pieces, prisoners decomposing in shit. History, I mean."

"It's terrifying," the investigator. "And also I feel guilty."

"Don't be frightened. Don't feel guilty. We exist. We can do what we need because we risk being killed. So you have to know it's worth it. Dying for it. If you have to. There are a lot of us now, more and more of us. We're all sorts of people, some of us cycled back from other sides, the sides we're fighting against. Appearances are deceptive, we can be anybody, we can be invisible. Invisible, Inc. is just part of it. We have surprising resources, some cosmic. No link in the chain is indispensable. You never know when it's going to happen. You just know there is a third force and you're part of it."

He gave the investigator an up thumb, walked off. The investigator drove back to the Boulderado, How waiting in the lobby.

"Red is dead," How.

"You mean red or dead?"

"No. Red. Dead."

From the look on How's face the investigator knew it was the red head from Invisible, Inc.

"I just saw him. How?" the investigator.

"Yes."

"No. How killed?"

"Bullet. No clues. Vaca want to see you."

Vaca at his garage took him outside to the junkyard fence.

"Golden just bought a rain forest," confidentially. "I heard it from Lena. Somewhere in Colombia."

"So?"

"Don't you see?"

"No."

Vaca looked exasperated. "Pharmaceuticals. They have drug prospectors down there, those forests are gold mines for new drugs. They must have found a cure."

"For what?" the investigator.

"It don't matter for what. If they found it it's a gold mine. It could explain the whole Latin American connection."

"There is no cure," the investigator. "I can already see your ghost."

"What's that mean?"

The investigator didn't know what that meant, he was surprised he'd said it. But now he'd said it it started making a certain amount of sense. He could see Vaca's ghostly double, he'd been noticing it for a while. Vaca's ghost was a rotting fence post fronting an inclined mountain valley. And now he thought about it it wasn't only Vaca, it was almost everybody, it was a new way of looking at people. Seeing the way they'd seem after they were dead. Not their bodies. Almost everybody had a ghost and the investigator for some reason was aware of it it spooked him.

Maybe because you're already a ghost. Lazonga.

"Seems to be a lot of ghosts around here anymore." Vaca was saying. "Anyway he's due here any time. Speaking of the devil."

Golden got out of a black Lexus car phone in hand. "Tell him in twenty-four hours or else," hanging up, "how's my SL 380?"

"Just about done now."

"Just about done now for a month. What's the problem?"

"I said," Vaca. "Parts."

"I'm going to be out of the country for a week, when I come back I expect to drive that thing out of here."

"Where you heading this time?" Vaca.

Golden's ghost was a glistening turd covered with flies in an empty field, the investigator could 'see' it, it was a metaphor but that was the closest the investigator could get in words.

"I've got a little something going in South America," Golden. "And come to think, cowboys are very useful down there. We need to clear the territory, clear it out and open it up. Just like the old West. It's manifest destiny all over again. Change the flora and fauna, pacify the natives. How about it?"

"How about what?" Vaca.

"Cowboys have always been good at this stuff. Buffalo Bill, Indian killer, no coincidence he's a national hero."

"You want to start all over again down there," Vaca.

"Well, they've never done it right. We've got to finish the job before they can go ahead and develop themselves. Get out of the Third World. NAFTA's a start. We're going to harvest that whole region, plants, animals, minerals and people. Think about it."

"I'm thinking. I'm thinking Sand Creek and Wounded Knee," Vaca.

"Yup," Golden. "The Wild West."

Back at the Boulderado he got out his laptop and checked his e-mail there was a message, "This is a chain letter the bucks stop here. Pass it on. A man in Minneapolis didn't and came down with rabies. A man in London didn't and came down with Mad Cow Disease." He didn't. There was also a message from Lenna or Lena, she'd started referring to herself that way it had become a joke between them that was the way she wanted to handle it. Her i.d. Invitation to dinner at her place, he'd never been there before. Since he was now in love he knew it would be a new ball game.

A large condo with plate glass looking up at the huge red cliffs they called the Flatirons. He complimented her on the apartment.

"It is one of the nicer units," Lenna or Lena. "You've changed, you look like you need sleep. Come on in to the living-dining area."

A fire was boogeying in the fire place, a large black cat roamed poker faced through the living-dining area. She was dressed in black, a black robe of a dress that tended to fall open in strategic spots. She uncorked a bottle of wine, they smooched on the couch, she micronuked a pre-pre-pared supper. The subject of conversation was the destructive force as against the creative force but it wasn't very interesting. Her opinion was that the destructive force was as legitimate as its opposite and anyway was bound to win out. Entropy. She kept citing examples from oriental theology which he didn't appreciate or maybe understand, the Roaring Dragon and the Singing Phoenix, "Lavigne says atomic energy is a dragon and phoenix, that's why they need to mutilate the cows."

"They? Who?"

"To see if their organs are being contaminated. By Rocky Flats. Theirs and ours."

"That's humane."

"Humane isn't the ticket. Lavigne says they want to know whether pre-irradiated beef preservation is more economical than post slaughter irradiation."

But then she started using sexuality as dragon-phoenix illustration he got off on another track, the sex track, soon the discussion was completely derailed. They began making love on the couch but as he was about to penetrate he felt something sharp tear at his balls. The cat was yowling and clawing at him.

"He's jealous," she laughed, petting the cat. He'd lost his erection and felt apologetic but she instructed him to forget the cat and lick her pussy. Since he was now in love he got down on the floor and did what he was told.

"Not there," Lenna or Lena. "A little higher. A little to the left. No, no, down a bit. Goddamit, no, you're still off, try to feel it. Good, yes, yes, that's it but harder, suck a little, not too hard, oh shit you lost it again, what's the matter with you? Can't you feel anything?"

The investigator suddenly sat up, his face wet. "Fuck this."

"You're not stopping?"

"What does it look like?"

The cat was still on the couch, she picked it up under the belly and flung it at him. It hit him on the side of the head, a furry bomb exploding claws. At that moment he saw her ghost, it had the shape of a large, pale mushroom, rags of tissue hanging from the shaft, bits of grainy matter freckling the blob of its top, tan on beige, gills on the underside implying drastic porosity.

Sitting on the floor next to the couch, scratched and dazed, the cat fled, he noticed a silver dollar on the glass end table. He was about to ask but she was glaring at him, legs together, her open robe gathered at her crotch. The black cat arched its back in a corner and hissed. He picked up the silver dollar and frisbeed it hitting the cat on the side it yowled and jumped away. She started clawing at him, he grabbed her wrists.

"What are you sitting there for?" screeching, "Get out. Now."

"Now wait a . . ."

"Go!"

"All right I'll do it." Since he was in love.

"You'll . . ."

"Lick it," the investigator.

"Who says I'm going to let you?"

"Please."

"Well . . ."

"But in the bed room," the investigator. "And no cat."

"I'm sorry about the cat. But you have to remember I was an abused child."

"What's that got to do with the cat?"

"I can't stand seeing cats mistreated."

"Who mistreated you?"

"My father. And my older brothers. Later when I got hooked on it, because you can be forced to have pleasure and then you want more, even my baby brother, I used to make him lick my pussy when nobody else was around. Pleasure is as pleasure does, or rather, pleasure does as pleasure was."

He got down to it in the bed room but there was a smell and it wasn't her smell. The word patchouli came to mind he didn't know what patchouli smelled like but if he had to put a word to it that's what he would have said, something sickly sweet, funereal, decadent, something he recognized and then he remembered what. Lavigne's smell. He came up, "You've been fucking Lavigne here? Him too?"

"He made me."

"How made you?"

"They make me do what they want," Lenna or Lena.

"They?"

"They pass me around. It makes me crazy. I don't know who I am sometimes."

"Why don't you get out of it?"

"Too late," Lenna or Lena.

"Why too late?"

"Because now I like it that way. They make you do it, and then they make you like it. Total domination. The tortured incorporates the torturer, that's the way it works. It's a protective mechanism. Then emulation, master-slave relationships proliferating in infinite variation and repetition."

"But I love you," the investigator.

"I love you too but what does that get me, with a quarter a free phone call."

"Try 911."

"Yeah."

He left. He decided he had to rethink being in love. He called Vaca for Lenna or Lena advice, he told him she was a death trip, "You knew that."

"So what do you do?" the investigator.

"Death is a bull you got to ride," Vaca. "Knowing sooner or later you fall off."

As soon as he got off there was a call from the desk, "There's an Inspector Derringer down here for you."

In the lobby the inspector led the investigator to some easy chairs in a corner. The inspector was dressed in different shades of grey, grey sports jacket, grey tie, his shirt was grey. His hair was greying and he had a greyish face, even his voice seemed grey.

"We're not accusing you of anything," the inspector.

"Good because I didn't do anything," the investigator.

"But that doesn't mean you're not under suspicion."

"For what?"

"For being around. Wrong times, wrong places. You want to explain?" the inspector.

"Coincidence." The investigator. The investigator caught sight of the inspector's ghost surprised because it wasn't grey, it was an acid green puddle in an arid landscape.

"In my business nothing is coincidence," the inspector.

"That can make you paranoid."

"I'm paid to be paranoid, paranoia solves mysteries."

"If all you're looking for is a solution, right or wrong," the investigator.

"You know a Dr. Greul?"

"I've heard of him, he's a veterinarian."

"We think he's bringing in illegal animals," the inspector.

"Animals?"

"Exotic animal traffic. We have reason to suspect you know something about it."

"No."

"We also know this area has become a center for smuggling musical instruments," the inspector.

"What instruments?"

"Organs, for instance."

"Don't know," the investigator, "but I hear there's brisk traffic in illegal insects. Bugs, for instance."

The inspector picked up his hat, a grey fedora. "We're watching you."

"And listening to me?"

The inspector left, the desk clerk beckoned to the investigator, there was a message for him from a Libby, at Invisible, Inc. Lobe in the hospital, he wants to tell you something urgent.

The investigator got to the hospital a little too late, Lobe was dead. He was still in bed, he looked rather well actually except his mouth was open. Still, or rather no longer. Out of time. For a flick of a second the investigator got a glimpse of time. It was invisible, and he could only see it by its flow that was leaving Lobe behind. Maybe that's what Lobe wanted to tell him, that even though he was late the investigator was still in time.

The investigator tried to see Lobe's ghost but couldn't. Maybe only the living have ghosts while the ghosts of the dead have died.

A couple arrived at bedside, they looked so much alike they had to be brother and sister, then the investigator recognized them as the twins he used to make love with. He greeted them but it was clear they didn't know him, which made him feel like a ghost.

"Relatives?" the investigator.

The male, "Our father's best friend."

"Your father is here?"

The female, "Dead."

"Have we met?" the investigator.

The female, "I don't live here. He does."

"What does he do?" the investigator.

"I work for Mort Gage."

"What's that?"

"He runs the MortGage Company," the male. "We handle DNA patents."

"Did you know him well?" the investigator, nodding at the corpse.

The female, "No. He had something we wanted."

"What?"

"We don't know," the male. "He was going to tell us."

They had a zomboid quality, both of them. Blank eyes. And they moved too slow.

"Who told you?" the investigator.

"Dr. Lavigne, from the University," the male.

The investigator kept trying but couldn't see their ghosts. It was a relief in a way.

"You both know Lavigne?"

The male, "She doesn't, she's from out of town."

"But I work with Dr. Greul," the female. "In Vail."

The investigator looked at his watch. He was almost out of time, the twenty-four hours was almost up. It was a little scary. It was more than a little scary, it was frankly threatening. Especially since the investigator had been informed time was more on time in Boulder than anywhere else. That was because of the atomic clock they had here at the Bureau of Standards that was the standard for time everywhere else.

Time is a form of radiation. Lazonga in his head again.

He decided to leave the hospital and find Vaca. The male and female were still with the body of Lobe. He had the feeling they were going to do something to it but he was in a hurry.

Going down the corridor the investigator met Ella who had disappeared from Lobe's house but she didn't recognize him when he stopped her.

"Where are you going?" the investigator. "Where've you been?"

"Lobe," Ella. "I was told to come."

"He's dead."

She looked appalled, then tears zagged down her cheeks. "He was supposed to give it back."

"What back?"

"The dream. He said it was like a mortgage and I'd get it back."

"Lobe?"

"No, Lavigne."

It was odd, she looked the same as before but was no longer sexy. No affect. No ghost. And she had the same zomboid look in her eyes as the male and female in Lobe's room, the same stupid hang to her jaw that on second glance wasn't stupid but something else. Something that made you think of them in the most generic terms. The male. The female.

He found Vaca at his shop in a good mood. He'd just gotten a dealership.

"A car dealership?"

"No a religious dealership, sort of. It's a new kind of mountain bike manufactured by a Judeobuddhist monastery funded by Golden. Karmic Cycles. What they sell comes back to them. After I get my cut. But if the medicine show project pans out I just might sell the shop."

"Medicine . . ."

"My friend that raises goats who gave me your address in New York. He's selling goat glands on the health food market. Don't ask me, all I know is he's raking it in. Old Western tradition. Snake oil. You know, I didn't recognize you at first, you change something? put on some mileage?"

"Not that I know of. You give up on cows?" the investigator.

"Just a fallback plan."

"What are goat glands for?"

"Mostly sex," Vaca. "You going to Golden's Halloween party up in Vail? He told me to ask you."

"It's not Halloween."

"Doesn't matter, it's whenever Golden wants it to be. Halloween used to be the big public fiesta here before it got rough. Now it's discreet private parties."

"Costumes?" the investigator.

"The theme is death and conquest. But as long as people don't recognize one another. We don't like witnesses in these parts."

"I thought I was your witness."

"Think again," Vaca.

When the investigator left the garage it was already dark. He'd forgotten time had changed when he came from New York and hadn't set his watch back, or forward, fall forward spring back, didn't know whether he lost the hour or was it two and whether it counted as minus or plus his allotted twenty-four. He realised he'd lost track, too scared to keep track. What scared him was that someone was. In the parking lot at the Boulderado a large bat came screaming towards him, veered off at the last second. Better check in with Invisible, Inc., Lazonga in his head, time for the treatment.

He parked in the Boulderado lot but before he had time to reach the hotel a bearded biker type got in his way, stocky, a bandanna on his head, punched him in the stomach the investigator doubled over. "This is a warning," the biker, hitting him again in the side, "This is another warning," kicking him in the groin, in the ass, slugging him in the kidney, "The last warning," kicking him on the ground twice in the head. "Back off," he disappeared, the investigator got up, made for the hotel, sat down in the lobby, bad headache, sign of concussion he knew. Derringer again, looking at him dubiously.

"Is that you?"

"No," the investigator.

"You look beat. I been waiting for you," the inspector. "We know what your girl friend is up to and we're ready to pick her up."

"If you know what she's up to it's a helluva a lot more than I know."

"This is no time to be coy," the inspector. "She's involved in some kind of graft."

"Why don't you let me in on it?" the investigator.

"Skin graft. You don't know she's been stealing trade secrets."

"Which trade?"

"The skin trade. We need your testimony. We already have Golden's and Lavigne's, she doesn't know yet."

"Sorry."

"She says you're the mastermind and you made her do it. It's you or her," the inspector.

"Then I guess it's me."

"Why?"

"Call it love."

"I'll be back, sucker," the inspector.

Up in his room the investigator opened up his laptop and checked his e-mail. There was a message on it that said, "This is a chain letter from the ddeadd break the chain. Pass it on." It was from chance@hell.invisible.edu. The double d's in dead made him suspicious. Was he delirious? Or did the dead make typos? Or were the ddeadd a little different from the dead? Or was this happening in his head?

He sent an e-mail to Lenna/Lena, "What they do with slaves is sell them down the river. Golden turned you in. Time to break your chain."

The investigator decided to take the advice of Lazonga in his head and hustle over to Libby's, catching a ride with How. How looked at him curiously when he picked him up at the hotel room. "You get haircut or something?"

How's ghost was odd, a Chinese character dancing in mid air like a marionette. The investigator recognized it from the I'Ching as Pi, "Holding Together."

"I just put my bet on a losing horse," the investigator.

"Why you do that?" How.

"I felt like it. That's something no chain can brake."

"Not intelligent," How.

"You do what you can," the investigator.

How told him there'd been a breakthrough. "Maybe we know who doing cow."

"Yes?"

"Mind engineering. Is a fraction of MortGage Co. Maybe do mind control gene implant in cow, then patent and graft into humans installing artificial intelligence. Eyes soon go dead. Called American Dream Corpse. Owned by Golden."

"You mean Corp?" the investigator.

"That correct. Is think tank where Lobe worked."

"What did he do?"

"He thought. They data base American Dream, for mind wranglers."

"What's a wrangler?" the investigator.

"Don't know. Something cowboy. What the American Dream?"

"Breaking the chain."

Libby was standing in her reception room reading a book when the investigator arrived. She had one hand up in the air as if she were holding something. There was a poster of Vaca on the wall that said, "WANTED: DDEADD AND ALIVE."

"I'm trying to stop the bleeding," Libby, looking up at her hand. "Pricked," she nodded at it. "But I'm used to deal-ing with pricks."

"Who pricked it?"

"You mean the latest prick? Hard to keep track but the bleeding seems worse this time. I'm a bleeder. I see you're morphing."

"Morphing?"

"You look different, you lose weight? pass a few birthdays?"

"Some say I've always been shifty. For example, I could fall in love with you," the investigator.

"[I'm free, remember Libby's short for liberty. B]ut I'm already carrying the torch."

"So what, so am I. Who for?"

"Vaca," Libby. "But I want him alive. The dead are gone. The ddeadd are doubled, going but still alive. Vaca knows the tallest tale, the winning of the West. It's a critical mess and could start a chain reaction that would blow things open if he told the truth. But the bastard's dying from the neck up and won't listen to me."

"Because?"

"He thinks I'm a mirage. But I'm not a mirage I'm a hologram."

He peered at her looking for her ghost but maybe she was her own ghost. Maybe that's what a mirage was. But he understood her, he could see loving Vaca. He himself was still in love with Lenna or Lena, maybe even Lazonga, as well as with Libby.

She led him into the treatment room, there was a massage table, a dentist's drill and a lot of computer equipment. Libby, "We're going to abduct you. Take your clothes off."

"All off?"

"Everything. And lie down."

"What's wrong with me?"

"Nothing. It looks like you're becoming what we call a clairvoyant crazy. Also known as an unhappy medium. But remember, you can always call me up. On the web. I'm linked to http://rtmark.com and http://altx.com."

The investigator did as he was told. He'd heard the abduction stories though he'd never believed them. But he knew they always involved being undressed.

She unhooked the dental drill and buzzed it a few times, testing, then disrobed her robe under which she was naked. "It's more effective this way," Libby, "this way we can harness the power of erotic energy."

He'd thought of her as ethereal but her body was technically flawless, hemispheroid buttocks solid and quivery, fullerdome breasts with nipples vectored up at a forty-five degree angle relative to the horizon. High flex elastic thighs, long easy torque waist, belly stretched taut indicating interesting plasticity characteristics, pubic fuzz promising infinite fractals of pleasure, good specs all around, well put together. Definitely not supernatural, maybe cosmic. Are E.T.s cosmic? he wondered.

She fixed his wrists in manacles attached to the table. His cock was immediately heavy but curved.

"We have to get the correct angle," Libby, and began to massage his groin area. It rapidly reached ninety degrees, "Good," she started the drill, "Open."

"Open what?"

"Mouth, it won't hurt. We just need to plug you in."

"You sure you know what you're doing?"

"No worry. Things seem chaotic but nothing's left to chance. Once a long time ago you turned left instead of right to look over your shoulder and the result was the rest of your life. Little things like that start a chain reaction that lock you in, though you couldn't have known. Scary, huh?"

"Why are you plugging me in?" the investigator.

"To break the chain and link you up. So you can get out."

"Out where?"

"Into another space," Libby. "Deep space. But we need your signature."

"My hands are cuffed."

"Your DNA signature. The invisible link in invisible ink in which everyone's story is written. Ghost story as well as detective story, soap opera or horse opera. The thing is to get beyond all the stories. Most people just change their story but can't get into deep space the mental jungles the unknown waste lands the dark matter where the stories stop. I can't. Maybe you can. Depends on your signature."

"Isn't this a little uh, mechanical?"

"It's tech but it's wellness tech," Libby.

"Who are you?"

"Let's say, a cosmic daughter of Dr. Frankenstein."

She turned on the high speed water cooled drill, quickly excavated a filling in his lower left molar, inserted a plug attached to an ultra fine cable, pulled a toggle on an electric panel. He felt an irresistible sensation in his groin, felt it coming from way off down the track, closer, closer, unbearable, then it hit him as his body spasmed and great gouts of sperm shot out of his tumid penis.

"We got a gusher," Libby. She rang for an assistant, a nurse came running in, "We got to cap this thing," yelling, the assistant scrambling for the appropriate equipment, "before it explodes."

Great geysers of hot sperm were gobbing the floor, sending the two women into dangerous skids as they tried to move fast. The investigator was assailed by screaming bats flapping around his head, himself screaming and groaning. The nurse got a condom over his jerking organ while Libby hit the toggle. When things calmed down the nurse took the condom into the lab to check his signature. She came back in a while, it could have been a couple of hours, or minutes, or days, he couldn't tell.

"The signature checks out," the nurse, he suddenly realized she was Athena Chipmunk, Hunch's friend, whose side was he on what were the sides?

"All right!" Libby. "He's our boy."

They hustled him to the airport. "Vampire bats," Athena explained. "There's a Multitech project down there in the upper Amazon. Ugly bloodsuckers but they secrete an anti-clot substance could be critical in organ transplants. Good comes from bad, bad from good, the old stories don't apply, that's what happens when you walk into the jungle."

Next thing he knew he was on Avianca into Lima. Lazonga met him on his way out of the airport. At least she looked like Lazonga but she was Spanish. And younger.

Maybe Lazonga was Spanish. Maybe it was Lazonga but Lazonga younger, Lazonga some years ago. Or maybe she was another of his conscious hallucinations. He thought she was dead but maybe she was ddeadd.

"Grim weather," Lazonga, waving toward the overcast sky. "They call it garua. You look different too. Think of me as a ghost." In the taxi more grim passing businesses and buildings guarded by security with uzis and flack jackets, some with turrets and machine guns.

"The guerillas," Lazonga. "And the criminals." He noticed she didn't have a ghost, maybe she didn't have a ghost because she was a ghost. People without ghosts made him real nervous. Either they were ghosts, which was okay, ghosts were okay with the investigator he was starting to feel like a ghost himself. Or sometimes, if they weren't mental mirages, they were just meat minus mentality, what he thought of as rogue entities, basically aliens of isn't-ness who could do anything no matter how revolting. Even animals had ghosts, even bats had ghost bats.

On the avenues it was mugging a go-go, no one interfered as a large thug ripped the pocket off an old man's shirt and casually mounted a bus with his wallet.

"It doesn't bother you?" the investigator.

"Don't forget I'm dead." A grim chuckle.

"Are you or aren't you?" The investigator felt he was starting to lose his bearings.

"You decide."

He tried to find out what he was doing in South America but she wouldn't say, she didn't know. But she said it was after she went into the jungle that she became a medium.

"I need to get my bearings," the investigator.

"There are no bearings. You're moving into deep space. The jungle is deep space."

Next day they were on a plane for the Amazon. He noticed the steward crossing himself as they gathered speed on the runway. Over the Andes the plane took a sudden dive, passengers screaming. "Don't scream, pray," the woman next to him yelling. The plane bounced back up the woman praying loudly. He had the impression they were entering a realm of pure chance where everyone had already given over control to the mercy of coincidence. An impression reenforced at the Iquitos airport where the baggage claim procedure, everyone running around at random agitated by heat and confusion, resembled the molecular chaos of Brownian motion. Now and then people got their bags but it seemed pure coincidence.

Boarded an odd three wheeled vehicle covered with an awning, a motorized rickshaw called an autokar the only kind of vehicle in town, inaccessible to freight from the rest of the country except by air. Whizzed along streets through turbulent traffic flow reminding the investigator of bumper cars.

Iquitos was a rotting monument to the rubber boom, richly tiled nineteenth century town homes moldering among tenements roofed with corrugated metal shimmering in the heat, a section of thatched houses on stilts and filthy houseboats on the Amazon. A river town, a jungle town, it conjured for the investigator the wildness and excitement of a raw frontier.

There was something ambiguous about the hotel, a little seedy, Lazonga said it was the best in town. The desk clerk was too good looking. He was vending an illegal ocelot skin to a drunk Texan the Texan said he wanted it, he knew how to get it in to the States, but he kept trying to tell the clerk about Baby Jessica stuck down a well, "The whole country geared up to save that little girl, you never heard of her?" The investigator asked the barkeep if they had a Glen Mackchrankie, they didn't.

Lazonga was withdrawn, strange. She didn't communicate much. "You know I'm a fortune teller," Lazonga. "I talk about the future. The present is boring, it's what we already know."

They got a ride on a river bus, an overcrowded hulk vintage African Queen, Indians, produce, cattle, Lazonga could understand the Spanish but mostly it was jabber in various native tongues. The Amazon was brown and miles across with a surface wrinkled like elephant skin, the investigator had the impression he could step off the boat and walk to land though he knew the still, shallow look hid speed and vast depths. Huge trees floating down, islands of vegetation adrift in the current. Dug out canoes slid along the edges of the rain forest which had the texture of a macroscopic turkish towel seen by a flea, tufts, loops, twisting threads, a silhouette of radically erratic flats and highs like musical notes.

"What I'm going to show you is the future," Lazonga. "What you have to keep in mind is that it's better than street kill."

"You're talking the exotic animal trade? musical instruments, organs? What?" as if he hadn't already guessed.

"It won't stop there," Lazonga. "There are more species per square meter in this jungle region than anywhere on earth, by far the most of them unknown. And you know who owns them, the MortGage Company, they just concluded a friendly merger with Multitech which bought a large hunk of jungle from the government. So who gets to say what lives and what dies off?"

The investigator didn't answer.

"They'll have more power than anyone since God," Lazonga. "And what I can predict definitely about the next century is we'll have a new American Dream, a dream of justice for some and inequality for all, dedicated to the denial of unhappiness. That much I can see as clearly as I see you in front of my face."

"How do you do what you do?" the investigator.

"I tune in to waves in the chronosphere. Time is just another form of radiation. Like x-rays. Both can reveal, both can kill. Try it."

"What do I do?"

"You have to de-focus. To begin to see what others don't. To become a medium for it. A monitor. Just like a CRT."

After a night and most of two days down river toward the borders of Colombia and Brazil, green parrots clattering overhead, pink dolphins bobbing up like tongues or toes, thatched villages above muddy banks, they climbed into a dinghy landing at a forlorn clutch of stilted huts, sullen Indians in jeans and shirts, children trying to sell them things repeating "Dollah, dollah," every child carrying a tiny pet monkey or baby armadillo or something. Picked up an Indian guide and moved off along a jungle path soon no path except that hacked by the guide's machete, vines hanging from tree tops, roots the size of oil pipe lines, trees on spidery stilts, trees oozing rubber, short thin trees, massive trees bare to a hundred feet up, trees.

Three o'clock in the afternoon still hot, but not as hot as he expected under the trees, but humid. The investigator limping from a bad fall over a trailing vine. Then it rained, hard and soaking, they stopped by a wide tributary, a tall tree undercut by the current tipped and fell slowly into the water as they watched. The rain stopped shortly but they stayed, soon heard a motor and a small launch nosed to shore. The guide left, they boarded, headed upstream. The pilot was not a native he carried a large automatic in a shoulder holster. The rain forest was peaceful, punctuated by colors of birdflash, small monkeys, hanging nests of jungle orioles and their dripping liquid calls, a sloth in a tree top, alligator eyes at water level watching.

In less than an hour they spotted a column of black smoke, a stench, slash and burn farming from what he'd been told or maybe they were clearing the jungle here too, the pilot wasn't answering any questions. They left the smoke behind, soon came to a wooden landing, a neat set-

tlement, corrugated metal roofs, something about the layout reminded the investigator of summer camp, there were
adolescents playing soccer in a field but in an odd way.
They were moving too slow.

The Texan from the Iquitos hotel came out of one of the
bungalows with a police dog on a short leash. "I don't know
why you're here but somebody wanted you to see it. They
say you have to make up your mind." He was carrying an
automatic weapon surprisingly small, his ghost an empty
mirror.

"About what?" the investigator.

"I just follow orders."

"About what?"

"This is our new facility," the Texan. "It's meant to crush
the cost out of the operation and deliver a superior product. With street kill you never know, you have to do a lot of
expensive tests and even then . . ."

"What is this place?" the investigator.

"It's an old leper colony. They say Mengele hid here a
while."

"You ever use that thing?"

"I'm a Texan. I shoot with my mouth. Here comes the
Doctor."

De-focus, Lazonga in his head.

The Doctor, bald and rimless glasses, Germanic accent,
zipping up his fly. Behind him on a cottage porch a barely
adolescent girl and two boys appeared to be copulating
slowly on a mattress.

"We encourage sex here as much as possible. Doctor Greul," extending his hand, the investigator looked at it as if it were a dead fish, it was quickly withdrawn. "Ach, don't be so quick to judgement, it's the best option open to them. Many of them would be dead on the streets by now. They all have terrible stories. Here their stories stop. So here they have several good years."

Re-focus, Lazonga in his head. There was a wormlike albino organism not a ghost but real with groping tentacles floating over Greul's left shoulder. Do you see that? Lazonga in his head.

Yes, I have double vision, the investigator in his head. What is it?

It's his real form, he's not human. He's an alien in a humanoid phase, Lazonga in his head.

"What do you do here exactly?" the investigator.

"We're a farming industry," Greul. "It's just supply and demand. There are a lot of people who want to turn their biological clocks back and have the money to pay for it. They say time is money my friend and this is just a matter of time. You control time you control everything, isn't it so? As for our young pets, they're glad to be here."

"Like Mengele's twins?" the investigator.

"Mengele was of course purely destructive, a maniac. I, on the other hand, was sponsored by the U.S. government. They brought me over and put me to work in Roswell, New Mexico, in 1947. They were interested in my experiments in trans-species infection. Here we keep them healthy, we have to. This is a strictly rational operation. Here Josefina, here girl."

A little girl jogged slowly over, maybe fourteen, strange stare, dilated pupils. The Doctor grabbed her lower jaw opening her mouth, "Look at this set of teeth, perfect." He thrust his hand in pulling out her tongue, "The color couldn't be better. She's yours if you want her," giving her a swift pat on the ass propelling her toward the investigator, who ignored her.

"How long do they stay?" the investigator.

"Very variable. It depends on the need for fulfillment."

"Need for whose fulfillment?"

"Order fulfillment. Right now we have a backlog and we're running low on inventory, but only on certain parts. They are, however, parts that need to be fully ripe for culling. And of course we need to minimize waste for parts not in demand."

"What do you do with parts not in demand?"

"Some we can freeze and warehouse." Nodding toward the column of smoke still visible above the trees, "The rest go to the crematorium. We think a lot about efficiency because this is a pilot plant. If it is profitable enough there will be many like it."

"How do you do it?"

"No problem, they go to sleep like little rabbits. I understand this may shock you, but who needs these children, who wants them? What you have here is simply the logic of our civilization addressed with clarity and maximum compassion. You accept it or you don't, but if you don't then go live on some other planet where humans are not a surplus product."

"What he's saying, partner," the Texan, "is do you want to live in this world or some other?"

"Some other." The investigator.

"This is not the end of the world," the Doctor, "we must not exaggerate. In this jungle there used to be cannibals, some say still are. You know why, basically it's a form of population control, simply the ecology of the food chain in conditions of scarcity. We are making some little scientific experiments in this direction."

"I don't want to hear it," the investigator.

"I can understand your reservations. Especially if you're a vegetarian. But otherwise, well, you have to taste it. You'd be surprised. Some people compare it to veal, others to pork. It's good! Once people get used to the idea it will be very marketable. It's already secretly test marketed in some places, people can't tell the difference. There's no point being snobbish about it when whole populations are starving to death."

"How often . . ."

"It depends on item velocity in the spare parts ware-house. It's costly to keep inventory on the shelf too long. So with our new microwaves . . ."

A putt-putt sound from the sky amplifying and soon a large helicopter appeared over the trees.

"The new shipment," the Doctor. "Selected in their prime from the last roundup. You will see the condition of these children and then you will realize what we do for them."

Young kids staggering and blinking off the helicopter, filthy, ragged. The last one off was the Colonel, herding them toward a barbed wire enclosure, shaking hands with Greul, saying "Clean them up, delouse them, and run them through the irradiation showers."

"It's time to go," the investigator. "The story is over."

"What story?" Lazonga.

"Our story, all of us. Maybe our time is over."

The investigator pulled a gun, he didn't even know he had one, squeezed the trigger, the Colonel's head exploded like a watermelon.

"Whoa!" the Texan, grabbing the investigator's elbow, the Texan had the gun the investigator felt it against the side of his head. "They said you had to make up your mind. So I guess you made it up. That means you made up ours." He was hustled to the edge of a clearing behind a tree, he heard Lazonga scream and a bang that was more like a blow to his head that was more like a silence that was more like time exploding into space.

What happened? He didn't know. The investigator didn't even ask where the helicopter was going, or when. He grabbed Lazonga and climbed on. It took off very quickly, he asked the pilot where they were headed but he didn't speak English he didn't speak Spanish he only spoke some Slavic language maybe Russian. The investigator felt he was launching into the void and didn't care, the green blanket of the rain forest spreading flat in all directions to the horizon, featureless except for an occasional gleam of water.

"So?" Lazonga.

"So what?"

"What are you thinking?"

"I've stopped thinking, what's the point? I've just become a Judeobuddhist, I've started practicing."

She gave him a look. "I may be dead, are you dead too?"

"I'm not dead, I'm cosmic."

Back in Boulder it was Halloween, he rented a skeleton costume for the party. He'd grown a white beard in the Amazon, lost weight, looked exhausted and limped as if slightly crippled. Time was erratic in Boulder it seemed, despite the atomic clock in the Bureau of Standards. People got old in big jumps sometimes acquaintances wouldn't recognize one another from one day to the next because the altitude kept you unnaturally young while the thin air's ultraviolet radiation could age you suddenly, the Shangri-la syndrome of high mountain climates. But the Amazon, when he walked into the Amazon he thought it was for a few days and when he walked out he was ten years older. How said nobody would recognize him anyway, but the investigator said the skeleton costume was time's x-ray of the human condition.

"Very gloomy," How. "Everything happening to you at once."

"That's always the way things happen, we just usually don't notice." He couldn't explain what happened in the Amazon, even to himself. His feeling was somehow he'd been raped, somehow he'd become cosmic. He felt he needed something like Judeobuddhism and didn't have it.

Drove up I-70 under the Divide through the Eisenhower Tunnel to Vail a mirage of condos metastasizing at the foot of the mountain. Skiers everywhere, early snow, striding in unlatched plastic boots like Frankenstein on vacation.

Golden's apartment was huge but curiously tacky, somebody's mirage of luxe gone to gilt mirrors, gilded woodwork, gold trim furniture, gold lamé cushions, glitzy light fixtures over persian rugs. Someone took his coat, he went in to the living room preoccupied with dark thoughts, stopped dead, the girls serving drinks and things were completely naked except for high heels, tawny skinned, Asian, under fifteen from the look of their bodies, some prepubescent.

He saw a male hand reach for a cunt, the girl stood in place squirming trying to balance her tray as the guest, in clown costume, picked an hors d'oeuvre with his other hand and popped it in his mouth. A man in mafioso get-up had one of the girls pulled down on his lap fondling her breast, her look impassive. Sicilian face, flashy suit, open shirt, gold cross, he could have been the real thing. Cowboys were plentiful, the investigator couldn't tell whether they were in costume or not. Several ET's wandered through. There were a lot of zombies around, some dressed in peeling bandages like Egyptian mummies, some with flesh partly eaten away, all walking around with a dazed look. A black bat stood immobile, spread wings flapping slightly. A small band of braves moved across the floor led by someone looked like Hunch, a long spear in his left hand, no doubt Chief Left Hand. A Conquistador stood nearby surveying the scene legs spread lance planted on floor red cross on chest, despite a visored helmet the investigator was sure it was Golden. He was holding a golden leash at the end of which a naked little girl with a dog collar around her neck.

The golden girls threading through the fantastic company with their offerings up for random grabs looked uncomfortable with more persistent advances but submitted, they must have been paid well.

A girl dressed in nothing but golden skin came by with a tray of champagne, he took a glass tossed it down grabbed another. Daniel Boone and Buffalo Bill were chatting with Geronimo nearby. The Marquis de Sade grey wigged with whip leash-led a low cut manacled Justine whose billowy Eighteenth Century skirts were pinned open to expose lashmarked buttocks. A dominatrix pulled two male subjects on neck chains, a man in leather steered a white slave by a cord attached to her pierced nipple. There were several vampires around, male and female, whose costumes implied a variety of unwholesome sensual tastes and, on the side of bestiality, a few dogs including a couple coupling in a corner doggy style attracting a casual crowd of the curious, but the basic mood in the room seemed to be boredom.

"This turns you off, doesn't it," a black cat, female.

"How can you tell?"

"Body language. And it also turns you on."

"Is my body saying that too? Maybe it's just arguing with yours."

"Don't worry about it, it turns everybody on at some level, it's biological. That doesn't mean you have to give in to it."

"To what?"

"To what? To human nature. Every man wants a slave girl. Every woman loves a Nazi."

"Not my bag," the investigator, drifting away. Halloween as psychodrama, a familiar voice in his head. Where had he heard it?

A crowd gathering at one side of the room, something happening on a low stage. The investigator floated over, Lenna or Lena, body covered only by Madonna corset and black net stockings, gold cross suspended from neck, arms on chair rump in air a look of blissful capitulation living out who knows what fantasy, or whose, as a man in blackface mounted the stairs to her.

The investigator caught a glimpse of the Conquistador at the other side of the room. He wasn't even looking. He was playing poker with a cowboy, an ET and a mafioso, a stack of silver dollars in front of him. The investigator walked over to him, "I guess you feel you can buy anything with those," gesturing toward the silver dollars.

"Why not?" the Conquistador, "it's a free market, isn't it?"

At the end of the room there was a tent set up with a sign: "Sexual Tourism." Inside past the tent flap he could see a chain moving rhythmically, what was attached to it obscured in shadow, a line of men waiting outside. A barker invited him to join the line: "It's libertine, it's liberated, and best of all it's free."

"I prefer not to," the investigator.

Vail unveiled, the voice in his head. Now he recognized it, the voice was his own.

Someone tapped him on the shoulder, "Time is up," Fenster's voice. Dressed as a black bat, a vampire bat judging from fangs.

The investigator could guess what Fenster was there for but felt oddly indifferent. He thought he'd become cosmic but maybe he was merely dead? He wondered where he might have died, he thought it was in the rain forest. With different luck he knew it could have been in the German camps or the Cambodian camps or in ex-Yugoslavia or in Ruanda but what's the difference? Whether he'd actually been there or not? More people died in those places than you think, the voice in his head, his own, some didn't even know it. Or at places like Wounded Knee and Sand Creek, you didn't have to be there to have died, you didn't even have to have been alive yet. They're still happening. A lot of Americans are born dead and don't know it, the voice. That's why the born again movement, resurrection the only hope.

The investigator knew this line of thought was sick but he was sick. Maybe he was dead. Maybe he'd been shot in the jungle. Anyway it was tiresome to think about.

"I have to show you something," Fenster. "You look tired."

"What's the rush?"

"You crosscountry?"

"In Maine."

Fenster led him to the basement of the house where they changed, picked up ski things, dumped them in a wagon, drove out of Vail on I-70 east. The investigator was getting very tired. Vale of pain, the voice.

"Where we heading?" the investigator.

"The Divide." South toward Keystone, past it, then east again and up on a snow rutted road, big flakes floating down.

"Why?" the investigator.

"Another storm coming in," Fenster. "We have chain laws in Colorado, you've broken the chain laws. You ever hear about the snow bats?"

"The . . ."

"Snow bats. Only come out when it snows, giant bats. Two foot wingspread they say. But white against the snow so you can't see them. People they find dead from exposure, skiers, snowshoers, hikers, they say it's really the snow bats. They can smother you with their wings, or freeze you, their wings are cold. Or just suck your blood till it stops flowing."

Fenster pulled out a small bottle of J.D. "A little antifreeze?" Each drank.

Fenster, shaking his head, "A few drinks of that and you'll start seeing those black helicopters."

"Helicopters?"

"You know, the black helicopters they say are flying round at night chewing up cattle. Talk about tall stories."

The road got steeper, unplowed but the wagon had four wheel. Wind was up, now and then it whited out, Fenster slowing to near nothing, stuck his head out and followed the embankment. "We're almost there."

"Where?"

"Montezuma. Beyond there's a trail head leads up to the Divide."

"Why Montezuma?"

"Who knows. Maybe it's named after Montezuma's revenge."

A forlorn collection of a few houses, wooden buildings ramshacked close and one log house inn. For visitors, the inspector wondered why there'd be any. He noticed a sign for a heliport, thought it strange. They stopped at the inn, Fenster told him to wait, went in, came back out with Vaca.

"Howdy, pardner," Vaca, "going for a little spin?"

"Going to see the snow bats," Fenster.

"Oh," Vaca. "The snow bats."

"What are we doing here?" the investigator, nobody said anything but he didn't really expect an answer. He was getting more tired every minute, wondered if he'd been drugged, felt disengaged as if he were here through some vast coincidence having nothing to do with him. Except it did.

"Is that what you had to show me?" the investigator.

"What?"

"The bats," the investigator was feeling less and less curious, out of dread, or maybe some kind of mental fatigue.

"Have another drink," the investigator took the bottle and pulled a long one. The road was untracked now, almost not a road, a part of a white duned desert disappearing under snow-shagged pines.

Several miles beyond Montezuma they stopped in a field blanketing out into whiteness and lost in curtains of falling and blowing snow.

"Good skiing," Fenster, they got out and onto their skis, pushed off into the frigid blank, "You'll warm up," Vaca.

The investigator couldn't see the car behind them, he could barely see his companions, their tracks filled up almost immediately. And he didn't warm up, he kept getting colder, his fingers especially.

They skied a while, Fenster breaking trail, herring-boning up hill, occasional kick and glide, the investigator wasn't very good at this he wasn't used to this kind of deep, powdery snow. Every once in a while he fell, it was like sinking under water with nothing to hold on to, they had to help him up.

"Still cold?" Vaca.

He wasn't, or he was but he didn't feel it. And tired, his legs, his arms from balancing on the poles, cold sweat drenched his body.

"Let me have your glove," Fenster. "The left one."

"Why?" he gave him the glove. Fenster tossed it into the blowing snow.

"The Divide is up that way," Fenster. "Head for it till you see the snow bats."

"Ciao muchacho," Vaca.

Trench and Vaca disappeared into the snow curtain.

The investigator was already beginning to shiver. He'd wanted to head down hill toward the car but after a while realized he'd been skiing up hill. His left hand was cruelly painful then went numb. He suddenly wasn't holding his ski pole any more, looked but couldn't find it, quickly lost his balance and fell into the powder, after a long exhausting effort managed to get up again. Skied a bit, fell again, at least it was warmer down in the powder.

It took him a long while finally he got up again. This time he was plodding through sand, up and down dunes, he'd always been attracted to the desert but was phobic about mirage. At first he thought the white Arabian was a mirage but when he got up onto the saddle he knew it was not just unbelievable luck she happened to be there on the desert, it was coincidence or maybe the third force. And then he knew the truth, of course, coincidence was the third force, the random beyond the stories where nothing is predictable, everything possible because everything is happening at once. That everything was happening at once, he understood that that was the message, that warning that he was just the worthless medium for. That was when he realized everything was going to be all right.

Invisible white bats were flying round his head, ghostly, menacing, but the Arabian outran them and soon the wagon came into view. Vaca and Fenster were taking cover behind it, ready to shoot. The inspector grabbed the rifle from the saddle slinging himself under the belly of the horse as she circled around the wagon, Vaca and Fenster firing he got off two quick rifle shots and they crumpled. But the horse was hit, she rolled over in the sand legs galloping in air, he loved her but knew he was going to have to shoot her. He ran his hand through her mane patted her muzzle then blew her skull apart she went limp. What had to be done had to be but she didn't die pointlessly because now he would be able to get back and warn them, that was the important thing.

He started the wagon and headed down the road as fast as he could. Soon he was on I-70 heading east. Back toward the city. He had to get word to them, there was still time, climbing the steep grade toward the Eisenhower Tunnel, into it, under the Divide, the long tube lit like a hospital corridor and through to the other side and there, he knew he'd finally made it, he was going to win, because spread out in front of him was the skyline of Manhattan and he heard singing as he entered the city, the filthy streets somehow beautiful, the beggars radiant, the homeless at home, the city at ease it must have been Sunday, a Sunday in early fall, the air crisp, the sky blue, boys playing in the streets as a song in a raspy voice filled the avenues and drowned the traffic noise, an old cowboy tune from another era:

> Git on lil dogies
> You're warm an you git fed

Don't stick yer stray necks out
Don't ask what's up ahead

I minded my business
An worked hard for my keep
But all the time I knew
I was dying on my feet

I made my heart cold
As the cruelly blowing snow
Numbed to the horror
I didn't want to know

Look into the mirror
Of this unseeing eye
Now dead to the roundup
That ends the dusty drive

Git on lil dogies
Go round an do your best
The rich lead the slaughter
The poor will git the rest

Go round lil dogies
Until the final grave
An let love save
Whatever love can save.

The RONALD SUKENICK Edition

Cows was first published in 2001 as an ebook by the Alt-X Press, Boulder, Colorado. A print-on-demand paperback edition was published in 2002.

Invisible Starfall Books is proud to publish *Cows* as volume 07 of its Ronald Sukenick Edition which is intended as a series of re-publications of the author's books in "definitive" editions. Each book in the RS Edition is carefully proofread and typeset.

Printed in Great Britain
by Amazon